THE TREASURE CHEST

·CHEST·

No. 3
Jewel of the East

DISCARD

by Ann Hood
Grosset & Dunlap
An Imprint of Penguin Group (USA) Inc.

GROSSET & DUNLAP
Published by the Penguin Group
Penguin Group (USA) Inc., 375 Hudson Street,
New York, New York 10014, USA
Penguin Group (Canada), 90 Eglinton Avenue East, Suite 700,
Toronto, Ontario M4P 2Y3, Canada
(a division of Pearson Penguin Canada Inc.)
Penguin Books Ltd., 80 Strand, London WC2R 0RL, England
Penguin Group Ireland, 25 St. Stephen's Green, Dublin 2, Ireland
(a division of Penguin Books Ltd.)
Penguin Group (Australia), 250 Camberwell Road, Camberwell, Victoria 3124,
Australia (a division of Pearson Australia Group Pty. Ltd.)
Penguin Books India Pvt. Ltd., 11 Community Centre,
Panchsheel Park, New Delhi—110 017, India
Penguin Group (NZ), 67 Apollo Drive, Rosedale, Auckland 0632, New Zealand
(a division of Pearson New Zealand Ltd.)
Penguin Books (South Africa) (Pty.) Ltd., 24 Sturdee Avenue,
Rosebank, Johannesburg 2196, South Africa

Penguin Books Ltd., Registered Offices: 80 Strand, London WC2R 0RL, England

Text © 2012 by Ann Hood. Illustrations © 2012 by Penguin Group (USA) Inc. Published
by Grosset & Dunlap, a division of Penguin Young Readers Group, 345 Hudson Street,
New York, New York 10014. GROSSET & DUNLAP is a trademark of
Penguin Group (USA) Inc. Printed in the U.S.A.

Cover illustration by Scott Altmann. Map illustration by Meagan Bennett.
Typeset in Mrs Eaves and Adelaide.

Library of Congress Control Number: 2011043283

ISBN 978-0-448-45469-6 (pbk)   10 9 8 7 6 5 4 3 2 1
ISBN 978-0-448-45473-3 (hc)   10 9 8 7 6 5 4 3 2 1

ALWAYS LEARNING   **PEARSON**

• CHAPTER ONE •

The Blond Woman

Maisie and Felix Robbins watched out their third-floor apartment's kitchen window as one of the biggest Christmas trees they'd ever seen was unloaded from a truck. Thanksgiving was still a week away, but Newport, Rhode Island, seemed to be skipping that holiday and racing right toward Christmas. On Bellevue Avenue, white lights twinkled from lampposts and fences, and wreaths hung on the doors of all the stores. In front of a restaurant on Thames Street, Santa sat in a sailboat pulled by eight leaping dolphins. And at Elm Medona, the mansion where Maisie and Felix lived with their mother in the old servants' quarters, a team of people had arrived to put up decorations, including this gigantic tree, which would sit in the Grand Ballroom.

"The one at Rockefeller Center is bigger, I think," Maisie said, squinting her eyes against the bright November sun.

Felix wasn't sure. But he said, "Absolutely," because to his sister everything in New York was bigger and better than here. Ever since their parents got divorced and they'd moved from their apartment on Bethune Street in New York City to Newport, Maisie had spent most of her time either homesick or scheming to get back. Felix, on the other hand, had started to feel at home in Newport. He had grown to love the smell of the salty air and the sound of buoys clanging on the wharf. The sight of sailboats in the bay on a sunny day looked beautiful to him. He had even started to enjoy eating seafood, stuffed quahogs and fried scallops and fish and chips. In fact, if their father lived with them instead of in faraway Qatar, life would be pretty perfect.

From their perch at the window, Maisie and Felix could now see oversized, gold ornaments getting wheeled inside.

"Gauche," Maisie said, enjoying the word. She loved using words that most twelve-year-olds didn't know. Like this one, which meant crude.

She wondered where those ornaments, too big for even this enormous tree, would get hung. Another truck arrived with piles of evergreen boughs. A blond woman in a camel-colored coat stood in the driveway directing all the workmen.

"Let's go see what they're doing," Maisie suggested.

Before Felix could answer, she was slipping on her sneakers and heading out the door. Felix followed his twin sister, as usual.

"Well now," the Blond Woman said, frowning up from her clipboard at Maisie and Felix. "Where did you two come from?"

"Up there," Maisie said, pointing.

"And what were you doing up there?" the Blond Woman said. Her hair was cut in a bob, and she looked like she'd spent too much time in the sun. Maisie thought she had a nose like a pig. And beady, blue eyes.

"We live here," Maisie said.

"I don't think so," the Blond Woman snorted.

"Well," Felix added, "on the third floor."

The Blond Woman knit her overplucked eyebrows into a scowl.

"Phinneas Pickworth was our great-great-grandfather," Maisie said, standing up straighter and trying to sound rich.

"Humph," the Blond Woman said.

Two men navigating a giant wreath decorated with enormous pinecones and gold ribbons hesitated in front of her.

"That one goes on the front door," she said, checking something off on her clipboard with a purple pen.

She glanced at Maisie and Felix again. "Did you *want* something?" she asked.

Felix shook his head.

"How long does it take to put all this stuff up?" Maisie said.

"In twenty-four hours, Elm Medona will be transformed into a Christmas wonderland. Just in time for all the holiday activities," the Blond Woman said, studying her clipboard.

"What kinds of activities?" Maisie said.

"Oh, all kinds of things," the Blond Woman said distractedly. "There are a few weddings. Lots of Christmas concerts and some kind of Victorian party. And of course the big VIP Christmas party on the ninth."

"You mean Elm Medona is going to be crawling with people for the next month and a half?" Maisie said, trying not to panic.

"Basically, yes," the Blond Woman said.

A dolly loaded with poinsettias rolled past.

"Pink? Pink poinsettias?" the Blond Woman shouted. "No, no, no. The pink ones belong at Rosecliff. Elm Medona gets the red ones." She scurried over to the men with the plants, waving her clipboard at them.

Maisie looked at Felix. "With people all over the place, we'll never be able to get into The Treasure Chest."

He could tell how upset she was. But a feeling of relief washed over him. When they had first moved to Elm Medona, they got a tour of the mansion. The docent showed them a secret staircase hidden behind a wall on the second floor. At the top of the stairs was a room called The Treasure Chest. It smelled like the Museum of Natural History and was filled with curious objects: maps, seashells, peacock feathers, a small, gold telescope, seedpods, an arrowhead, a porcupine quill, a compass, a bouquet of dried flowers, and hundreds of other things.

One night they sneaked back into The Treasure Chest and found a letter dated 1864. When they both yanked on it, they got carried back in time to the childhood farm of Clara Barton. Clara had told them how she'd nursed her brother David back to health after he fell from a barn rafter, and they'd listened to her father tell stories about his time in the Indian Wars. The next time, they landed on the island of Saint Croix with Alexander Hamilton and stowed away on a ship to America with him. Even though both trips had been grand adventures, Felix was afraid to time travel again. Their great-great-aunt Maisie made them promise they would do it one more time, but the more Felix thought about it, the more he worried they might be pushing their luck. What if they didn't get back home? What if they were stuck in the past?

Maisie had no such worries. She couldn't wait to get back in The Treasure Chest, pick up an object, and leave Elm Medona and the twenty-first century behind.

"Well," Maisie said as she watched the Blond Woman point an angry finger at the men with the poinsettias, "I guess that means we'll just have to do it tonight."

⼟   ⼟   ⼟   ⼟   ⼟

Maisie loved her mother's bacon and egg pasta more than almost anything. The real name for it was spaghetti carbonara, but Maisie liked her name for it better. Her mother fried bacon nice and crispy, tossed it with spaghetti and Parmesan cheese, and then added three beaten eggs to it.

Before the divorce, she added four eggs, and this small detail made Maisie sad. When Maisie walked in the kitchen, she smelled bacon cooking and saw her mother beating eggs in the green-striped mixing bowl. She grinned. They would eat. Their mother would go back to her law office at Fishbaum and Fishbaum. And then she and Felix would go to The Treasure Chest.

"Perfect," Maisie said out loud.

"I count my lucky stars every day that you two never get tired of spaghetti carbonara," their mother said.

Felix did not love spaghetti carbonara, mostly because he didn't like eggs. They were slimy. But beaten like this and mixed up with the cheese, he could almost forget there were eggs in it. Almost.

"Why so miserable?" their mother asked him.

"I . . . I wish you didn't have to go back to work," Felix said. He could practically feel his sister glaring at him.

"Oh, sweetie," their mother said, and tousled his hair.

"We could play hearts tonight," Felix said hopefully.

"Not tonight," his mother said. She pulled a strand of spaghetti out of the pot of boiling water and offered it to him. "Done?" she asked.

Miserable, Felix took a bite. "Done."

His mother studied his face. "What's going on?"

"Yeah," Maisie said evenly. "What's going on?"

"Maybe I just want to stay home tonight."

"You are staying home, aren't you?" their mother said, confused. She looked from Felix to Maisie, who smiled and shrugged innocently.

"I won't be too late," their mother added as she drained the pasta and began mixing it with the bacon, eggs, and cheese. "We'll play hearts tomorrow night. Okay?"

"Great!" Maisie said so enthusiastically that their mother actually looked at her suspiciously. "I love hearts."

Felix tried to eat as slowly as possible as if that might make their mother stay home longer. He couldn't help it. As the weeks and months had passed, Newport and their small apartment at Elm Medona felt more and more like home to him. Time traveling had scared him each time. But even more than ever, he wanted to just stay there and go to school and eat quahogs and play hearts. Besides, their father was arriving on Christmas Eve, and that was enough for Felix to look forward to.

But before he'd finished his last bites of spaghetti, their mother glanced at her watch and decided it was time to get back to the office.

"You two stay out of trouble," she said as she put on her powder-blue puffy coat and a pair of blue-and-white mittens.

Maisie smiled at her sweetly.

At the door, their mother turned to Felix. "Tomorrow night, buster," she said. "I'm shooting the moon."

He nodded and watched her as she walked out. The sound of her boots on the stairs faded, then disappeared.

"What is wrong with you?" Maisie hissed at him. "We *promised* Great-Aunt Maisie."

"I know," Felix said. He twirled and untwirled the spaghetti on his fork.

"So?" Maisie demanded.

"So I don't want to go, that's all. I want to stay right here. I like it here, Maisie. I like Miss Landers and my whole class and . . . and everything." When he saw the hurt look on her face, he said, "I'm sorry, Maisie. But I do."

"Without Dad?" she asked. Her bottom lip trembled like she was about to start crying.

"Of course not. But he'll be here soon and—"

Maisie blinked at him a few times, then took a deep breath. "Whatever," she said. "We have to do it for Great-Aunt Maisie. Not for me."

Her lie broke his heart, but he still wished he

could talk her out of it. "Maybe we could tell her we did it. We could pick somebody and say that's who we met. Like . . . George Washington? Or Abraham Lincoln?"

Maisie stood up. "You can stay right here if you want. I'm going to The Treasure Chest."

"Maisie," he said, "come on."

But she ignored him. She walked out the kitchen door without looking back.

"Maisie!" Felix called.

He ran after her, surprised that she'd already made it down the stairs. The first time they had gone to The Treasure Chest, they'd used the dumbwaiter in their kitchen that led to the Kitchen in the basement of Elm Medona. But now they knew where the key to the first-floor door was hidden, and they let themselves right into the dining room.

Maisie was already putting the key in the lock when Felix reached her.

She turned when she heard him. "I don't care if you come or not," she said, her green eyes blazing.

Felix suspected that for some reason the time travel only happened if there were two people. And those two people had to both hold an object from The Treasure Chest. He hadn't figured out all the rules exactly yet, but he felt pretty certain about these.

Maisie stepped into the dining room with Felix close behind. The smell of Christmas— pine trees and cinnamon—filled the air. The large dining room table that always remained set with the Pickworth china now had a dozen tall, red pillar candles wrapped with evergreen and pinecones in the center. Boughs of evergreen looped across the borders of practically everything: the side bar and serving table, the doorways and backs of chairs.

"Wow," Felix said, "the Blond Woman works fast."

A sense of yearning struck Maisie so hard that she let out a long, sad sigh. She thought it was possibly the longest, saddest sigh of her life so far.

"What is it?" Felix said.

Maisie looked at her brother. "I can't do it," she said.

When she saw the relief flicker across his face, she shook her head. "No, I mean I can't do the holidays. It's all wrong. Thanksgiving at the nursing home with Great-Aunt Maisie. And then Christmas with Dad staying at the Viking Hotel instead of with us."

"Mom said we'd all have Christmas morning

together," Felix reminded her softly. "Dad will make his eggnog French toast, I bet."

But Maisie just shook her head again.

She was thinking of her father dragging the Christmas tree up Hudson Street, she and Felix guiding him along. She was thinking of how, when they walked in the door, their mother always complained they'd chosen a tree that was too big. And how their father made them hang the tinsel one silver strand at a time.

"Even if we do go to The Treasure Chest," Felix told her as gently as he could, "we'll still have Thanksgiving at the nursing home, and Dad will still be in a hotel at Christmas." No matter how long they stayed in the past when they time traveled, it was as if no time at all had passed in the present when they returned.

"I know," Maisie said. "But somehow going back in time and meeting Clara and Alexander and who knows who else makes it a little better."

Felix's heart ached. Not just for Maisie, but for their family and all they had lost. He took his sister's hand and pulled her up.

"Come on," he said. "Let's go to The Treasure Chest."

The giant Christmas tree they'd seen arrive earlier that day now stood all decorated in the

Grand Ballroom. Wreaths, oversized pinecones, boughs of evergreens, and twinkling lights seemed to be everywhere Maisie and Felix looked. As they walked up the Grand Staircase, Felix paused as he always did at the black-and-white photograph of Great-Aunt Maisie as a little girl that hung on the wall. For the first time, he saw a glimpse of the Great-Aunt Maisie he knew in the eyes. *Funny*, Felix thought as he stared at the photo. When they'd arrived in Newport, Great-Aunt Maisie had barely been able to speak or walk. Now she was making her way down the corridors of the Island Retirement Center with the help of a walker and ordering around the staff as clear as anything. Every time she saw them, she asked about the details of their journeys with great interest. And she'd practically ordered them to go again. *Soon. You must*, she'd said.

"Come on," Maisie called from the top of the stairs.

A chill ran up Felix's back. He turned from the picture and gazed upward at his sister.

"Maisie," he said. "I think our time travel is . . . is . . ."

She tapped her foot impatiently. "Is what?" she said.

"Is making Great-Aunt Maisie get better," he said.

"That's ridiculous," Maisie said, even though he could tell she was considering the possibility.

"I don't think it's ridiculous," Felix said thoughtfully. "I think when we go back in time, so does she. I mean, she gets younger."

Maisie twirled a strand of her tangly hair around her finger, tugging on it as she thought about what Felix said.

"Is that why she wants us to do it again so badly?" she asked.

Felix nodded. "I think so."

"Well," Maisie said, breaking into a grin, "then we definitely have to do this. We're practically saving Great-Aunt Maisie's life!"

Unable to wait any longer, she walked down the hallway to the spot on the wall that opened to reveal the hidden stairway. But when she got there, she couldn't believe what she saw.

"Oh no!" she shrieked.

Felix came up behind her.

Right on the place they had to press for the wall to slide open hung one of those giant wreaths, decorated with gold ribbons and pinecones.

Maisie stared at the wreath in disbelief.

"Well," she said finally, reaching up for it, "we'll just have to take this gauche thing down."

Felix, knowing better than to argue with her, took hold of the bottom of the wreath as Maisie grabbed the side.

"Lift it on three," Maisie said. "One . . . two . . ."

Felix leaned his shoulder into the wall beneath the wreath for extra heft, ready to lift.

A voice cut through the air.

"What in the world do you two think you're doing?"

Without letting go, Maisie and Felix both turned their heads toward the voice.

The Blond Woman stood at the top of the stairs. She was dressed like a Christmas tree herself, in forest-green pants, a green turtleneck, and a red sweater tied loosely around her shoulders. Her hands were on her broad hips, and her beady eyes were narrowed menacingly.

"Don't. Move," the Blond Woman said.

Then she pulled a walkie-talkie from her pocket, lifted it to her mouth, and said, "Security! We have a break-in!"

· CHAPTER TWO ·

Find Thorne!

"Do I even dare ask what you two were thinking when you *broke in* to Elm Medona?" Maisie and Felix's mother said.

Maisie just folded her arms over her chest and stared back at her defiantly.

But Felix said, "We just wanted to see the decorations."

"We're invited to the VIP Christmas party on the ninth," their mother said. "You could have seen them then. Now look at the mess you've made."

Maisie and Felix looked. A team of security guards crowded into what used to be Phinneas's wife Ariane Pickworth's room—the very room she died in shortly after giving birth to Great-

Aunt Maisie and her twin brother, Thorne. The creepiest room in the house, Felix thought, despite its powder-blue walls and the ceiling painted like a sky with puffy, white clouds seemingly floating across it. It was near the scene of the crime, so the Blond Woman had hustled them inside to wait. First the security guards arrived, then four Newport policemen, then a man from the local preservation society, and finally their mother. The man was tall and balding with a big gut pressing against his purple fleece jacket. He looked annoyed; their mother looked really angry.

"How did you even get in?" the man from the local preservation society asked them. "I mean, it's impossible." The tip of his bulbous nose was sunburned, which was odd for November.

"We . . . ," Felix began. "Uh . . ."

Maisie broke into a grin. "We used the dumbwaiter," she said. No way was she going to reveal that they knew about the key on the first-floor landing. "First I put Felix in it and sent him down, then I followed."

Felix nodded enthusiastically.

"What did I tell you about playing in elevators?" their mother screeched. "Especially ancient ones! Especially something that isn't even meant for human transportation!"

Her face looked weary. *And why shouldn't it?* Felix thought. She worked a million hours a week and took care of them all by herself. Plus, she ran errands for Great-Aunt Maisie, who got more demanding the better she felt.

"I'm sorry, Mom," Felix said softly. He *was* sorry, too.

Even Maisie felt bad now. Their mother had smudges of mascara under her eyes, the hem on her navy-blue wool skirt was coming down in the back, and a small run crept from her heel toward her calf as if even her clothes were weary.

The Blond Woman hovered above Maisie and Felix now, her face all contorted and her beady eyes wild.

"I want to press charges," she said. She pointed at them. "I knew you two were troublemakers. I just knew it."

"Surely we can come to some appropriate punishment that's less extreme," their mother said. "They are only twelve years old, after all—"

The Blond Woman reeled around to face their mother. "Do you know how many valuable items are in this mansion? Do you have any idea?"

"But they haven't taken anything," their mother said.

"If we let them off the hook for this, who knows

what they'll do next! Set the place on fire? Paint the walls? Throw a party?"

"We didn't touch anything," Maisie said.

The Blond Woman's thin eyebrows shot upward. "You were attempting to remove a wreath," she said.

The man from the preservation society cleared his throat. "I think we can just deactivate the dumbwaiters and give the kids a stern warning that if they even place one toe in here, we'll have to discuss terminating the agreement with the family about those living quarters upstairs."

"Now wait a minute," their mother said, worry washing over her face. "It's my understanding that my aunt allows you to use this place in exchange for one dollar a year as long as she—"

"Exactly," the man said. "As long as *she* lives in the servants' quarters. Last I heard, *she* wasn't living there."

The Blond Woman smiled, victorious.

"Now," the man said, "if you don't mind, I'm going to go home. My wife is waiting for me. I want to go home and get to bed." He turned a hard gaze on Maisie and Felix. "And I suggest you do the same."

They stood up from the gold, brocade chair they'd been squeezed onto.

"See?" the Blond Woman said, pointing her chubby finger. "They got dirt on the fainting couch."

Everyone except the policemen leaned forward to inspect it.

"No, no," the man from the preservation society said finally. "I believe that's an old stain. A Pickworth stain."

Relieved, Maisie and Felix started toward the door with their mother. But the man stopped them.

"Mrs. . . . ," he began.

"Ms.," their mother clarified. "Robbins."

"I trust you won't leave the children unsupervised again?" he said.

She swallowed hard. "Of course not," she said softly.

With that, she placed a hand on each of their shoulders and steered them past the man from the local preservation society, the Blond Woman, the two policemen, and the team of security guards, then out of Ariane Pickworth's bedroom, into the hall, and down the Grand Staircase, not letting go of them for even a second.

⊥　⊥　⊥　⊥　⊥

Thanksgiving Day was gray and drizzly, the dreariest Thanksgiving Maisie and Felix could remember. Instead of waking to the smell of a

turkey roasting in the oven and finding their
father peeling sweet potatoes and their mother
trimming green beans, they woke up to silence and
the aroma of coffee that had been made several
hours earlier. Maisie padded down the hall to the
kitchen, where a note lay on the table: PICKING UP
CHAMPAGNE, CHESTNUTS, AND NIÇOISE OLIVES FOR
GREAT-AUNT MAISIE. BE READY TO LEAVE AT 11:30.
AND DON'T BUDGE!!!!!!!!!

Maisie sighed. She wasn't even sure what
Niçoise olives were. She just knew that Great-Aunt
Maisie demanded the most unusual things, all
the time. Even on Thanksgiving day. Maisie sat at
the table, miserable. When Felix appeared fifteen
minutes later, she pushed the note toward him.

"Happy Thanksgiving," he said hopefully.

"*Un*happy is more like it," Maisie said.

Just then the phone rang, and Felix answered
it, glad to have someone—anyone—to talk to other
than his sister.

As clear as if he were in the next room, their
father's voice boomed, "Happy Thanksgiving,
Felix!"

"Dad!" Felix shrieked.

"Is the turkey in the oven? Your mother always
underestimates how long it takes to roast a turkey,"
their father said wistfully.

"Uh . . . actually . . . ," Felix said.

Their father chuckled. "She doesn't have it in yet, does she?"

"Well, no," Felix said. "We're having lunch with Aunt Maisie. At the Island Retirement Center."

"That sounds depressing," their father said. "Can the old bird even eat?"

"Oh, she's doing much better, Dad," Felix said. "She walks with a walker now and bosses everyone around."

There was silence, then their father said, "That's impossible."

"Maybe it's a miracle?" Felix said. "A medical miracle." He had a pit in his stomach as he said it, afraid that he knew exactly what was bringing Great-Aunt Maisie back to health.

"Maybe," their father said.

By now, Maisie was practically jumping on the table to get Felix to hand her the phone.

"Maisie wants to say hi," Felix started to say, but his sister managed to grab the phone from him before he finished.

"Daddy!" Maisie said. "It's raining out, and Mom's not even home because she had to go and get all this gourmet stuff for Great-Aunt Maisie because the food at the assisted living place isn't good enough for her, and we have to eat with all those old sick people, and you're halfway around the world and—"

"Whoa, sweetie," their father said. "It can't be all bad."

"But it is," Maisie said.

The kitchen door opened, and their mother came in, her arms full of groceries.

"This is the worst Thanksgiving ever!" Maisie said.

Their mother's face seemed to crumple in on itself. She slowly put the bags on the counter and, with her back turned away from Maisie and Felix, began to unpack them.

Felix glowered at Maisie, but she just tossed her unruly hair, stretched the cord of the phone as far as she could, and disappeared with it around the corner.

"Do you think it's the worst Thanksgiving ever?" their mother asked Felix without turning toward him.

"Of course not," Felix lied.

The dining room at the Island Retirement Center was decorated festively, with straw cornucopias filled with plastic vegetables on each table, burnt-orange tablecloths and napkins, and a big papier-mâché turkey wearing a pilgrim's hat hanging from the main lighting fixture.

Great-Aunt Maisie believed in arriving late and making a grand entrance. So she made them all wait in her room until they would be exactly fifteen minutes late. She and their mother had a glass of champagne and some Niçoise olives, Great-Aunt Maisie freshened up her Chanel Red lipstick, and then they finally made their way to the dining room.

En route, Great-Aunt Maisie whispered in Felix's ear, "Where has your latest adventure taken the two of you?"

She was moving slower than last time he saw her, so he had a chance to explain without his mother, who was ahead of them by quite a bit, hearing him.

"The preservation society came in and decorated Elm Medona," he told Great-Aunt Maisie.

She rolled her eyes. "I bet it looks just dreadful."

"No, it's really fancy," Felix said. "But they put a wreath right over the wall with the staircase."

Great-Aunt Maisie came to a stop, her hands gripping the sides of her walker so hard they trembled.

"So take the wreath down. That isn't very difficult to figure out, is it?" she said.

"We tried," Felix began.

She slapped the walker, hard. "Tried? You mean you couldn't get it down?"

"I mean we got caught," Felix said.

Their mother had stopped to wait for them, and Maisie, who had stormed ahead of her, stopped, too, her eyes on Felix and their great-aunt.

"So try again," Great-Aunt Maisie hissed at him.

"We can't," Felix whispered. "They said that if we even set foot in there they'll kick us out."

"What? Who said that?"

"The preservation society," Felix told her.

"Is he slowing you down?" their mother said to Great-Aunt Maisie as she hurried to help her along.

"Oh, get out of my way," Great-Aunt Maisie said, pushing past their mother and then Maisie.

"Oh dear," their mother said. "She's in a foul mood."

土　土　土　土　土

The turkey was dry. The mashed potatoes were lumpy. The gravy wasn't hot. And they only served cranberries from a can. Maisie ate only the green bean casserole. Great-Aunt Maisie drank too much champagne. Felix ate some white meat but without any gravy. And their mother ate nothing at all until the pumpkin pie was served.

"This is the worst Thanksgiving I've had since 1922," Great-Aunt Maisie said.

"I am sorry," their mother said. "Maybe we should have had it at home."

"Humph," Great-Aunt Maisie said.

A woman in a bright-orange suit stood at a podium at the front of the room and spoke into the microphone.

"For those of you who don't know me," she said, "my name is Abby Bain, and I'm in charge of special events here at the Island Retirement Center."

There was a smattering of applause. Great-Aunt Maisie muttered, "Oh please," under her breath.

"I don't want to keep you any longer," Abby Bain said, "but I wanted you to know that the centerpieces are yours to keep. And to be fair, they go to the youngest person at the table."

Maisie and their mother both turned to Felix.

"Ha," Great-Aunt Maisie said. "So you're younger than your sister?"

"Well," Felix said, "by seven minutes."

Great-Aunt Maisie shook her head sadly. "Just like Thorne and me," she said.

"And one final thing," Abby Bain announced. "When you made your reservations for today, we put your names in this bowl, and one of you will be able to take this big tom turkey with you." She pointed to the papier-mâché one wearing the pilgrim hat.

"This is ridiculous," Great-Aunt Maisie said.

"The lucky winner," Abby Bain said, digging into a big fishbowl and pulling out a name, "is Maisie Pickworth. Where are you, dear?"

Their mother waved to Abby Bain. "She's right here!"

Great-Aunt Maisie frowned at their mother and at the people smiling at her for winning and at Abby Bain, who was already cutting the turkey down from the light fixture.

Then Great-Aunt Maisie's face softened. She looked at Felix and smiled. "Seven minutes younger," she said. "Just like Thorne and me."

He nodded.

"He has my shard from the Ming vase," she said.

"Maybe?" Felix said.

"Not maybe," Great-Aunt Maisie said.

The last time they time traveled, they learned that they needed to have a shard from a particular priceless vase with them in order to do it. Great-Aunt Maisie's piece, which she kept hidden in a

Fabergé egg, was missing. She believed Thorne had stolen it.

Abby Bain was grinning as she walked toward them holding the turkey. Their mother jumped up to meet her as she approached.

"So if you can't get into The Treasure Chest yourselves, the solution is simple," Great-Aunt Maisie said softly. She got to her feet and opened her arms for her prize. "Find Thorne. Get my shard back. And I'll just do it myself." Great-Aunt Maisie was grinning, too. "The preservation society can't keep *me* out of Elm Medona, can they?"

Abby Bain deposited the giant papier-mâché turkey into Great-Aunt Maisie's outstretched arms.

"Isn't he darling?" Great-Aunt Maisie said.

Slowly, she stepped away from her walker, just enough to dip into a stiff but elegant curtsy. As she rose, she turned her icy stare to Maisie and Felix and mouthed one word: *Thorne.*

·CHAPTER THREE·

The VIP Christmas Party

For Felix, it was a relief to stay out of The Treasure Chest. While Maisie schemed and plotted ways to get back into Elm Medona, Felix put time travel and Great-Aunt Maisie's orders to either do it again or find her long-lost brother, Thorne, far from his mind. Instead, he practiced for the upcoming spelling bee, went to the Jane Pickens Theater on Saturday afternoons with kids from his class, decided to run for student council, and spent his free time daydreaming about Lily Goldberg.

Lily Goldberg sat one person down and across from him in school, the perfect position for him to study her unnoticed. She was the smartest person in the class. And, Felix thought, the prettiest girl. Her dark hair was cut short like a pixie's, and she wore funny dresses from the vintage store with patterns of things like teapots or flamingos on them. Sometimes he got a faint whiff of mothballs from her. Lily was adopted from Hunan, China, when she was a year old. He knew this because she gave a report on it with a slide show of her adoptive parents in China picking her up. Felix loved the pictures of baby Lily, dressed in a purple snowsuit, staring at the camera all perplexed. He loved, too, that she still stared out at the world looking perplexed.

Felix had made a good friend at school. His name was Jim Duncan, and more and more Felix found himself going off after school with him. Jim Duncan liked going down to the docks and looking at all the sailboats, too. The only difference was that Jim knew a lot about sailing and could tell Felix stories about who owned which boats and which races they'd been in. His own father had done the Newport to Bermuda race six times, and Jim told Felix stories about storms and squalls his father had sailed in. Jim liked to read, too, and on cold afternoons they went to the Coffee Grinder on Bannister's Wharf and drank hot chocolate, looked out at the boats, and discussed the books they were reading. Jim Duncan liked postapocalyptic stories and Felix liked old novels, but it was fun to trade back and forth and to talk about them.

Of course all of this made Maisie extremely jealous. Once Felix invited her along, but all she did was scowl and complain that the scones tasted stale. Later, at home, she'd accused him of liking Jim Duncan more than he liked her.

"That's silly," Felix said. "You're my *sister*."

But Maisie stayed upset with him all night and the next day, too.

To keep Maisie happy that week after Thanksgiving, Felix told Jim he had to go straight home after school. He spent the afternoons with Maisie playing Rummikub and listening to her latest schemes for breaking into The Treasure Chest or finding Great-Uncle Thorne.

By the end of the week, he was forgiven.

☥   ☥   ☥   ☥   ☥

The student council elections were on December 8, and Felix went to school early to put up posters. He had worked on them most of the night before, writing "FORWARD WITH FELIX" in fat bubble letters on light-blue poster boards. The hallways were still dim when he arrived at Anne Hutchinson Elementary School. The early morning light cast a golden tone on the empty school that made Felix feel warm and happy. Mr. Hamilton, the custodian, must have just polished the floors because of the sharp smell of lemons and the high shine on the old wood. Humming softly to himself, Felix took the roll of tape from his pocket and began to hang the posters on the walls between classrooms.

From somewhere down the hall, he heard a soft whimpering. He paused and listened. Yes, it was definitely the sound of someone crying.

"Hello?" he called into the emptiness.

The crying stopped.

"Are you okay?" he asked.

No answer.

Felix walked in the direction the sound had come from. At the end of the hall, he saw that the light was on in the supply closet and the door stood ajar. Carefully, he pulled it open. There, among the reams of printer paper, lined paper, math paper, construction paper, and manila paper sat Lily Goldberg.

At the sound of the door creaking open, Lily looked up, her face wet with tears and her eyes puffy from crying.

But her voice was strong and angry as she said, "Get out of here! Now!"

Felix yanked the door shut, but he didn't walk away. Instead, he pressed his cheek to it and said, "What's wrong, Lily?"

"None of your business," she said, just as angrily. "Go away!"

He hesitated. "I can't leave you in a closet crying," he said.

"I'm not crying," she said, then began a new round of sobs.

Felix opened the door again. Lily had her face in her hands, her short, dark hair sticking up on her head and her short fingernails covered in chipped, baby-blue polish. She was wearing her dress with the teacup pattern and a pair of scuffed, black Doc Martens. Felix thought he had never seen a more beautiful sight. Except for the crying.

"Lily?" he said.

"What are you doing here, anyway? It's like seven o'clock," she said without looking up.

"Putting up my campaign posters," Felix said. "For student council," he added.

Slowly, she lifted her head. The smell of mothballs and fruity shampoo filled the air.

"What are you doing here?" Felix asked her.

"I don't want my parents to see me cry, so when I feel sad I come to school early and hide in here so I can cry in peace."

She glared at him.

"If you tell anyone about this," Lily said, "I'll kill you."

"Okay," Felix said.

He started to walk away, but Lily called after him. "Come back here," she said.

Felix did. When Lily moved to make space for him on the floor of the closet, he squeezed in next to her.

"Maybe you'll understand," she said thoughtfully. "I mean, you had to leave New York, right?"

Felix nodded.

"See," Lily said, her perplexed eyes gazing away from him, "I was born in China, you know? And my parents, the ones who adopted me, are great. They are. That's why I come in here to cry, so they won't hear me. I love them and everything. But I have this . . ." Her slender fingers plucked lightly at the front of her dress. "This *hole* in me. This *ache*."

Lily glanced at Felix as if to gauge his reaction. He nodded.

"I just wish I could go back there. To China. And see where I came from, you know? Maybe even see my birth parents." She paused. "You probably think that's totally dumb, right?"

"No," Felix said. "Not at all. My father lives

halfway across the world, and every day I wish I could see him."

"He does?" Lily said.

"Qatar," Felix told her.

She nodded, clearly impressed.

"Want some help hanging your posters?" Lily asked softly.

"Yes," Felix said. He stood and held out his hand to help her to her feet.

Side by side, they hung the posters along the sixth-grade corridor, outside the cafeteria, on the preapproved campaign bulletin board in the library, and on the gymnasium walls. They finished just as the first bell rang. By now, the school was awash with the sounds of students arriving, their voices and footsteps and locker doors slamming.

"Well," Lily said, slinging her backpack onto her shoulders. "See ya."

"Wait!" Felix said, not ready to let her go.

She turned her perplexed face toward him.

"We're having a Christmas party at our house tomorrow. Want to come?"

To his surprise, Lily didn't take any time to consider. Instead, she just said, "Sure," as casually as anything.

⚊ ⚊ ⚊ ⚊ ⚊

"You did *what*?" Maisie said angrily to Felix.

She couldn't believe that her brother had invited someone to the VIP Christmas party without even asking her if it was okay. And Lily Goldberg of all people?

"I like her," Felix said.

"Well maybe I don't!" Maisie snapped. Now Felix would be fawning all over Lily Goldberg at the party, and Maisie would be all by herself, miserable.

"She's really nice," Felix said.

Maisie flopped onto the sofa, her skirt puffing out around her as she did. They were both dressed for the party, waiting for their mother to emerge before they went downstairs. Maisie had on the chocolate-colored silk skirt she'd worn to bar mitzvahs last year and a black cashmere T-shirt. Felix wore khakis and a white button-down shirt with a clip-on red bow tie and a slightly too big navy-blue blazer their father had bought for him for those same bar mitzvahs. *You'll grow into it*, their father had said. Felix was still waiting for that to come true.

"I cannot believe my life," Maisie moaned.

Their mother appeared in the living room doorway. Maisie had grown so used to her in her work clothes, slightly rumpled suits in neutral colors and low heels, that she gasped when she saw her in a slinky black velvet dress, sheer black stockings, and high heels.

"Come on," their mother said. "I don't look that bad, do I?"

Felix grinned up at her. "You look gorgeous!"

She smiled her shiny, lipsticked lips. "You two dress up pretty nice yourselves."

"Do you know that he invited someone?" Maisie said.

"You could have asked someone, too," their mother told her.

"Like who? I don't have even one friend here."

"You will soon, sweetie. I promise," their mother said gently. "Come on. It's time to go."

On their way downstairs, Felix stopped to pick up something shiny on the landing between the third and second floors. The shard! Maisie must have dropped it when she'd raced upstairs earlier to get ready. He remembered her taking off her winter layers as she'd run, her scarf and then her mittens and then her puffy purple jacket. Felix held the shard in his palm for a moment. There was no time to go back up now and put it somewhere, and Maisie had no place to keep it in that outfit. He shoved it in his jacket pocket and caught up with Maisie and their mother on the next stairway.

"I so wish Great-Aunt Maisie could have come. Don't you?" their mother was saying.

Felix did not wish that at all. Every time they'd seen her since Thanksgiving, she'd pestered them to find Thorne. Or to go back into The Treasure Chest. *I'm losing my patience,* she'd told them just a few days ago.

"But she hasn't been doing so well lately," their mother continued. "Poor thing."

Felix got a heavy feeling, like he'd swallowed rocks. It was their fault Great-Aunt Maisie wasn't doing well.

They arrived at the bottom of the stairs on the first floor, exited the way they would if they were getting into their car, then walked around to the front of Elm Medona to enter.

White lights twinkled in every shrub and tree. Oversized wreaths hung on the enormous front doors where two red-uniformed butlers stood, ready to open them for guests. Shiny cars filled the circular driveway in front of the house and valets scurried to open doors and help elegant ladies and tuxedoed men step out. Standing there, Felix could almost imagine what it must have been like a hundred years ago, when Phinneas Pickworth threw lavish balls and people came from all over Newport and beyond, dressed in fancy clothes and jewels. Great-Aunt Maisie had told them that her father kept peacocks that opened their glorious tails almost on cue for guests. Often, the parties had themes: the White Party, where everyone dressed in white and ballerinas danced excerpts from *Swan Lake* for the guests; the Masked Ball, where guests wore elaborate costumes and masks and Phinneas Pickworth had jesters perform for them; even Night on the Nile, with women dressed like Cleopatra, snake charmers, and a real sarcophagus that Phinneas had acquired on a trip to Egypt was opened, revealing a shriveled mummy inside. *Seven of the guests actually fainted,* Great-Aunt Maisie had told them, her blue eyes shining with delight at the memory.

Maisie and Felix followed their mother inside. Immediately, butlers with heavy, silver trays filled with champagne glasses appeared. Their mother took one, her face glowing in the candlelight. The smells of a dozen different perfumes filled Felix's nose.

"Can we go find the buffet?" Maisie asked.

"Don't get into any trouble," their mother warned them.

"We won't," Felix promised.

Their mother disappeared in a swirl of velvet.

"Come on," Maisie said, clutching Felix's arm. "With so many people and so much excitement, no one will even notice if we sneak upstairs."

"No way," Felix said.

Across the Grand Ballroom, he caught sight of their nemesis, the awful Blond Woman. She had on a too-tight navy-blue gown that showed the small rolls of fat around her middle and pink lipstick on her thin, tight lips. Worst of all, her beady, blue eyes scanned the room as if they were lasers looking for Maisie and Felix.

"Look over there," Felix told his sister.

Maisie followed the lift of his chin. "Oh no," she groaned. "Not her."

"I have to wait for Lily," Felix said. "We'll meet you at the buffet."

Maisie's heart sank. Just as she feared, Felix would be with stupid Lily Goldberg, and she would be off on her own.

"Fine," she muttered, pushing her way through the crowd toward the dining room. Maybe, Maisie thought, she would just have to go up to The Treasure Chest alone.

± ± ± ± ±

"You *live* here?" Lily Goldberg said as soon as she found Felix in the Grand Ballroom.

"Not exactly," he said, blushing. "We live in an apartment upstairs. We don't even use this door to get to it."

"But it's a mansion, right?" she said, tilting her head back to stare at the giant chandelier.

"Well," Felix admitted, "yeah."

Lily tried to take it all in: the marble floor, the gold trim along the ceiling, the butlers and fancy people. She shook her head. "But why do you live upstairs?"

"My great-great-grandfather built Elm Medona," Felix said, feeling embarrassed. Maybe this was a bad idea after all.

Lily stood beside him, speechless.

"There's food," he said. "In there." He pointed in the general direction of the dining room.

"Okay," Lily said.

She had on a black dress with a big, red petticoat beneath it that made the bottom of the dress stick out and rustle noisily when she walked.

"You look nice," Felix told her.

Lily only nodded and looked more perplexed than usual.

The dining room table was heavy with food. A man in a tall, white chef's hat carved fat slices of beef. Shrimp glistened on silver platters. Long, thin spears of asparagus nestled beside slices of bright yellow and red peppers. Cheeses and olives and rounds of baguettes sat beside oysters and clams gleaming in their shells. Felix saw that the Pickworth china, with its interlocking, ornate *P*s, was actually being used.

"Why was your grandfather—" Lily began.

"Great-*great*-grandfather," Felix interrupted.

"Why was he so rich?" she said.

"Banking," Felix said. Then he added, "We're not rich. At all."

"Do you think *my* great-great-grandfather, I mean my Chinese one, was like an emperor or something?" Lily said.

"Maybe," Felix said. "Probably."

"Wouldn't that be something? If I went back to China and my great-great-grandfather was in a castle or something with servants and fancy things?"

Felix studied Lily Goldberg's face for a moment. She didn't look perplexed at all. Instead, her face was soft, her eyes dreamy. That was when he decided.

He took her hand. "I want to show you something," Felix said.

Felix and Lily stood in front of the green

wall on the second floor, right at the spot where,
behind the enormous wreath, he could press
lightly to reveal the hidden staircase. It had been
hard to get Lily up here because she kept stopping
to stare at the tapestries, the paintings, the
statues, the murals, and the furniture behind the
red velvet ropes. But finally they'd climbed the
Grand Staircase and arrived at this spot.

Felix glanced around to be absolutely certain
no security guards or wayward guests or the Blond
Woman were anywhere nearby. Satisfied, he
reached his hand through the wreath's greenery
until it hit the wall. Then he pressed lightly, and
sure enough, the wall magically moved and the
hidden staircase appeared.

"That is so cool!" Lily shrieked.

"Just wait," Felix said, motioning for her to
come along.

"A secret wall! A hidden staircase!" she said as
they climbed up the stairs. "You have the coolest
house ever!"

Felix unclasped the red velvet rope that hung
in The Treasure Chest's doorway. With a sweep
of his arm, he beckoned inside, where Lily's
shrieking and gasping grew even more intense.

"What is all this stuff?" she kept asking as
she picked up and then put down one item after

another. A feather. A round ball of alabaster. A
fountain pen. A locket.

"Phinneas Pickworth was a collector," Felix
explained.

He watched the curiosity and excitement in
her eyes, trying to decide if he dared do what he
wanted to do. After all, he had the shard in his
jacket pocket. If he and Maisie could time travel
by picking up an object, why couldn't he and Lily?
Imagine what she would think if he could take her
back to China. Felix knew that he couldn't find
her ancestors, but being there might make her
feel better, might fill that hole she'd described to
him.

Felix's eyes darted across the room, searching
for something that just might be Chinese. That
red lantern? The swath of embroidered silk? The
curved dagger?

"Felix?" Lily said, holding something out to
him. "Do you think this is from China? It's jade,
I think."

She held out her hand where a small, pale-
green box sat on her palm.

"Maybe," he said.

"I wonder if there's anything inside," she said.
"Like jewels!"

With her other hand, Lily opened the box.

"Dirt?" she said.

Felix nodded. The box was filled with nothing but dark soil.

When he looked back at Lily, there was something in her eyes that made his heart jump.

"Lily," he said quietly. "I want you to take this box and hold really tight to it. I'm going to hold on, too. And then pull on it. Okay?"

"Okay," Lily said slowly.

She put her fingers with their chipped, baby-blue nail polish around the jade box, her gaze steady on Felix. He put his hand on it, too, his fingers brushing right up against Lily's. Lily yanked.

The two of them stood like that for an instant, waiting.

A voice cut through the room.

"Felix!" Maisie exclaimed. "How could you?"

She stomped up to them, pushed Lily hard enough for her to lose her grip on the box, and glared at her brother.

"Maisie," he began.

But before he could say another word, Maisie grabbed the jade box filled with dirt and yanked, hard.

The room filled with the smells of spices, river water, and wet soil. A wind rushed past Maisie and Felix, carrying the sounds of voices and music. Felix caught a fleeting glimpse of Lily Goldberg's perplexed face. And then, they were gone.

· CHAPTER FOUR ·

Zhenzhu

Maisie and Felix landed with a thud.

Where are we now? Maisie wondered as she struggled to get her bearings. It was dark and smelled like the produce stand at the natural food market. She pushed her arms upward and struggled to the surface, moving the small, hard grains that surrounded her out of the way as she did. Was she in a sandpit? When her head popped out she came face-to-face with an old, wizened Chinese man. His face was weathered and deeply wrinkled, and his wispy, white hair was tied back in a pigtail.

The old man began to shout at her in Chinese, waving his arms and jumping up and down.

Maisie looked down. She had landed, she realized, in a giant basket of rice. That basket of rice stood next to many more baskets of rice, which stood in a row of small stalls selling vegetables. From her perch, Maisie could see green beans and radishes and green cabbages. What she didn't see was Felix.

Still shouting at her, the old man took her arm and pulled hard. Maisie tumbled from the basket in a shower of rice.

"I'm sorry," she said, getting to her feet and wiping dirt from her chocolate-brown party skirt.

The old man practically picked her up by the nape of her neck and carried her like a kitten through the crowded marketplace, Maisie's legs kicking the air in protest. He kept screaming at her until they reached the end of the market, where he deposited her harshly on the ground.

Maisie sat a moment, rubbing the back of her neck where he'd held on to her. In front of her was a riverbank and a muddy river with boats moving slowly along it. Some of the boats had white sails, others were painted bright colors. She smiled. They had come all the way to China! A surge of excitement coursed through her as she looked around. Men and women in cotton tunics and pants with triangular straw hats carrying small baskets of food passed, staring openly at Maisie and whispering to one another in Chinese.

China!

Slowly, Maisie got to her feet and went back into the marketplace. *Felix has to be in here somewhere. Doesn't he?* she wondered. Stalls lined both sides, and people haggled over prices in loud Chinese. The first stalls had piles of live crabs and high heaps of small silver fish and piles of ugly, flat fish. Next came stalls that sold glistening, brown ducks cooking on spits over coals, their long necks tucked against their wings. Maisie paused over the mountains of chilies—red, green, yellow, skinny, fat, round, long—and then at the baskets of spices. Cinnamon sticks and whole peppercorns, gnarly ginger root and clusters of purple garlic.

At the vegetable stalls, Maisie crossed to the other side of the market to avoid the old man whose rice she had landed in. Although she could recognize most of what she saw, she stopped and picked up a long, squash-type thing with a reddish-brown skin. The woman who ran the stall slapped Maisie's hand and took the vegetable from her, speaking rapid Chinese to her.

"Sorry," Maisie said again. Would she spend her whole time here apologizing?

The woman pointed to a row of the vegetables. She lifted one, pointing to the white interior dotted with holes. It looked like lace. Maisie understood that the woman was trying to convince her of its freshness.

Maisie nodded politely, then moved on, past red peppers and melons in all sizes and shapes and colors.

"Were you even going to try to find me?" Felix said from behind her.

For an instant, she forgot how angry she was at him for taking Lily Goldberg to The Treasure Chest and just felt relief that he was all right.

"We're in China!" she said with delight.

But then she remembered what he had done, and she spun around angrily, pretending to be fascinated with some watermelons.

"I landed in a cart filled with radishes," Felix said. "The woman selling them laughed so hard she cried when she saw me."

Maisie ignored him.

"She gave me some," Felix said. He opened his hand in front of his sister's face, revealing five pinkish-red radishes with skinny stems still attached.

When she didn't answer him, Felix said, "I just wanted to impress her."

"*Impress* her?" Maisie said, her eyes flashing angrily. "The Treasure Chest is ours. *Ours.*"

"It's just that she's—" he began.

But Maisie would have none of it. "You can keep your stupid radishes. In fact, you can do anything you want. Alone."

With that, she pushed him aside and joined the crowd in the marketplace, letting herself get carried along past yet more stalls until she reached the exit at the other end. Tears stung her eyes, but Maisie refused to give in to them. Felix had betrayed her. And she wasn't sure if she could ever forgive him.

Felix followed Maisie through the marketplace and out to the street, keeping a safe distance behind her. She had certainly been mad at him before. When they were six, she wanted a puppy, but their parents told them their apartment was too small. Felix took their side, and Maisie gave him the silent treatment for an entire night. When they were nine, she didn't speak to him for an entire week because he told their parents that she and Flora Mingus had taken the Staten Island ferry. Alone.

But this was different. The Treasure Chest was important to Maisie, and he'd gone there purposely without her. If the jade box resting in his pocket now had taken him and Lily Goldberg here, he would have been happy. Maisie seemed to know somehow that he wanted to leave her out. And now they were all the way in China, and she was trying to escape from him. If he lost Maisie here, he might lose her forever.

The street was lined with men cooking on woks perched on crates. Felix smelled chilies sizzling in oil, ginger and garlic, and fried fish. People squatted by the woks, eating with chopsticks from small, white bowls. Some of them stared up at him as he walked past. Others openly glared. He searched his mind for anything he knew about Chinese history. Was there a period when China and the United States were at war? Felix didn't think so. Without speaking Chinese, how would he ever find out what year it was?

At the end of the street stood a larger, busier one. Dazzled by all the action there, the colorful banners of silk flapping in the breeze, the red paper lanterns hanging above shop doors, and a seemingly endless array of jugglers, magicians, musicians, and puppeteers, Felix paused. As soon as he did, he lost sight of Maisie.

Panicked, he called her name.

The entire crowd seemed to stop moving and turned to stare at the skinny American boy in the bright-red bow tie and glasses with his cowlick sticking up.

"Maisie!" he called again.

A round-faced woman with a mole above her lip shook her finger in his face and reprimanded him in rapid Chinese.

"My sister," Felix said. "I can't find her."

Another woman, this one skinny and long faced, joined her.

"My sister?" Felix tried again, hoping maybe this woman spoke English.

But both women just continued to speak to him in rapid Chinese. Felix swallowed hard. He'd seen movies where angry mobs threw strangers into jail. Or worse. His eyes scanned the crowd for a friendly face, but everyone seemed to be frowning at him. Their voices sounded angry, he thought. Or was that just because he couldn't understand anything they were saying?

Felix appealed to the small crowd that had gathered around him.

"Does anyone speak English?" he asked.

"I do," someone said.

The crowd parted to let a boy walk through to Felix. He was as tall as Felix, dressed in a blue cotton jacket and trousers, soft, black cloth shoes, and a red hat trimmed with gold Buddhas.

The boy spoke to the crowd in Chinese, shooing them away. They moved back, away from him and Felix, but didn't leave.

Then the boy turned his attention toward Felix. To Felix's surprise, the boy had round, blue eyes. Despite his fluent Chinese, he was clearly American.

"I'm so glad you showed up," Felix said with relief.

"Oh, they're just not used to seeing Westerners walking the streets like this," the boy said. "In fact, they don't like Westerners very much at all."

He smiled at Felix in a way that made Felix relax a little.

"I'm here with my sister," Felix explained. "And I lost her in the crowded street."

"Ah," the boy said. "She can't go too far. After this street there's just fields and houses."

"Yíqiè dóu hên hâo," he shouted to the crowd. "Yû nî wû guáng."

Slowly, the people dispersed, still glancing over their shoulders as they walked away.

"Wow," Felix said. "What did you say?"

"That everything was fine and they should go about their business."

"How do you know Chinese like that?" Felix asked.

"I've lived here my entire life," the boy said.

He began to walk down the street, waving for Felix to follow him.

"But you are American, aren't you?" Felix said. He felt certain this boy would help him find Maisie.

"Well, I was born there," the boy said, clearly not pleased. "In West Virginia, where my parents come from. But I've lived practically my whole life here. My father's a missionary."

"What's that?" Felix asked.

"He came for the Southern Presbyterian Mission," the boy explained. "To convert the Chinese. He isn't having much luck, but he keeps trying."

"Oh," Felix said. "You mean convert them to a religion?"

"To Christianity. He thinks they're all heathens."

"Heathens?" Felix said. Maisie would know what that meant, but he wasn't sure.

"Someone who's uncivilized," he said. "Who hasn't converted to Christianity."

"Do you think that?" Felix asked.

The boy stopped, his blue eyes alert and certain.

"Oh no. Not at all. But don't tell my mother and father," he said, winking.

They were standing by several men writing

Chinese characters in thick black ink on white paper.

"Letter writers," the boy explained. "For the people who aren't educated. These men write letters for them."

Felix nodded, mesmerized by the graceful and intricate characters.

"What's this sister of yours called, anyway?" the boy asked.

"Maisie. She's taller than you, with kind of curly, blondish hair, and she's wearing a black T-shirt with a fancy, brown skirt."

"And what are you called?" the boy said.

"Felix. Felix Robbins."

The boy stuck his hand out. "I'm Zhenzhu."

They shook hands briefly.

"Very American, shaking hands, right?" Zhenzhu said, laughing.

"I suppose so," Felix said. "What do people do when they meet here?"

"You cup your left hand over your right, this high"—here Zhenzhu did this in front of his chest—"and then you raise your hands like this."

He lifted them slightly in the air.

"Like a salute?" Felix said, imitating him. He placed his left hand over his right and lifted them to his forehead.

"Yes! That's it," Zhenzhu said happily.

The two boys grinned at each other, and in that moment Felix knew: Zhenzhu was who they had come to China to meet. The jade box filled with dirt needed to go to him.

"In earlier times," Zhenzhu was saying, "it was customary to raise the hands as high as the forehead and to give a low bow. But we don't do that anymore. Now we ask, *Chī le ma*? Have you eaten?"

"*Chī le ma,*" Felix said slowly, the unfamiliar words clumsy on his tongue.

"Not bad," Zhenzhu said.

Zhenzhu scanned the crowd and shook his head. "I think your sister would stand out easily, don't you?"

Felix followed the boy's gaze. "Yes," he agreed, sighing. Despite Zhenzhu's confidence that Maisie couldn't go very far, Felix was starting to worry all over again.

"She either went toward the fields or toward the river," Zhenzhu said, clapping his hand on Felix's shoulder to comfort him. "Really, you can't get lost in Zhenjiang."

When he saw Felix's puzzled face he added, "That's where you are. Zhenjiang."

"Zhenjiang," Felix said softly.

"Let's go this way," Zhenzhu said, pointing away from the river. "No doubt she walked along the street here, and it leads this way."

"Zhenzhu?" Felix said as they moved past silk shops and tailors and stalls selling elaborate kites.

"Yes?"

"What's the date today?"

"December 9, 1899," Zhenzhu answered without hesitating.

"1899," Felix said. "In a few weeks it will be a new century."

Zhenzhu laughed. "Not here," he said. "In China, the New Year is in February, and it will be 4598, the Year of the Rat."

Felix was about to tell Zhenzhu that he had been to Chinese New Year's parades and feasts in Chinatown back in New York. But just then he caught sight of his sister's tangled hair up ahead.

"Maisie!" Felix yelled.

This time, she did stop. But she didn't return his smile.

"That's her," Felix told Zhenzhu.

"The unhappy-looking girl?" Zhenzhu said.

"That's the one," Felix said.

Maisie didn't take even one step toward her brother and the boy he was with. She just waited for them to make their way to her.

"How could you leave me like that?" Felix said immediately.

Maisie laughed. "You had every intention of leaving me back home, didn't you?"

"No," Felix said. "Not exactly."

Maisie glared at him, her arms folded across her chest defiantly.

"That doesn't even matter now," he continued. "We're here. In China. It's 1899, and we need to stick together."

Zhenzhu cleared his throat.

"Oh," Felix said. "Sorry. Maisie, this is Zhenzhu."

His eyes, she realized, were a vivid blue.

"You're not Chinese!" she blurted.

"I am in my heart," Zhenzhu said. "I've lived here practically my entire life."

"Without Zhenzhu's Chinese, I don't know what would have happened back there," Felix said.

Zhenzhu nodded. "It's true. These are difficult times for Westerners here. The empress does not like their interference. In the north there's been a lot of trouble."

"Are we safe?" Felix asked, worried.

"Here, yes. But my father has seen some disturbing attacks. His mission is up north. He carries a stick with him everywhere he goes to defend himself."

"From who?" Felix felt a shiver of fear.

"Westerners call them Boxers, but they call themselves the Righteous Fists of Harmony. Their goal is to rid China of foreigners." When Zhenzhu saw the look of fear in Felix's eyes, he added, "Don't worry. So far in Zhenjiang nothing has happened."

The words *so far* offered little comfort to Felix. He tried to catch his sister's eye, but she ignored him completely.

Despite her anger at Felix, Maisie felt excited to be in China. When her parents had first told them about the divorce, she had imagined running away—far away, to someplace like India or Argentina or China. And now here she was, right in the middle of China, and there was an empress and dangerous warriors and a blue-eyed boy with Buddhas on his hat and a bustling marketplace filled with kites and silk and food cooked in woks. She almost smiled.

Zhenzhu looked from Maisie to Felix. "But tell me, why are you two here? How did you get here?"

"Um," Felix said. "We're . . . I mean . . . we . . ."

"We came down the river on one of those boats," Maisie said.

"From Shanghai?" Zhenzhu asked her.

"Yes," Maisie said quickly.

He nodded. "That explains it."

"It does?" Felix said.

"Of course. Shanghai is not even really China. It's filled with British and Americans. It doesn't even *look* like China." He paused, concentrating. "But where are you staying?"

Felix shrugged.

"Have you run away from home?" Zhenzhu said, obviously delighted by the idea.

Before they could answer, he continued. "Yes! That's it! Your parents are dreadful, cruel people, and you two were kept prisoners in Shanghai. Desperate to see the real China, you snuck onto a boat and traveled down the Yangtze River to Zhenjiang. What an adventure!"

"Yes," Felix agreed, "we are having an adventure."

Zhenzhu clapped his hands together. "You'll stay with me!"

"Really? Will it be all right with your parents?" Felix said. But even as he asked this he knew that of course it would be all right. Zhenzhu had to be the person they were supposed to meet. He touched the jade box in his pocket. It was meant for Zhenzhu.

"My father's away all the time, anyway. And

Mother always takes people in. She likes a full house. Come on! Follow me. We'll go there now."

They walked past fields of cabbage, up a hill, to a small brick house with a covered porch in front. Roses climbed the walls, their vines thick with flowers. Maisie took a deep breath of the fragrant, floral scent. Large earthen pots of chrysanthemums in shades of yellow and orange flanked the front door.

"Mother!" Zhenzhu called when they entered.

A tall woman appeared. Felix thought she must have been pretty once, with her blond hair and high cheekbones. But her eyes looked so sad and her face so weary. She reminded him a little of his mother.

"These are my new friends," Zhenzhu said. "Maisie and Felix Robbins. They're American."

Her eyes lit up at that.

"Americans! Where are you from?"

"New York," Maisie said at the exact same time that Felix said, "Rhode Island."

Zhenzhu's mother frowned.

"We're *from* New York," Maisie said.

"But we moved and we live in Rhode Island now," Felix explained.

"My family hails from West Virginia," she said sadly. "I do miss home," she added, shaking her head. "The apples and berries. The clean grass and water."

"Mother," Zhenzhu said, "do you think you might give us some dinner?"

"Of course," his mother said.

"Thank you for having us, Mrs. . . ."

"Sydenstricker. You're quite welcome, Felix." Her voice grew quiet. "It's lovely to have more children in the house."

"What's for dinner tonight?" Zhenzhu asked.

"Wang Amah made your favorite."

Zhenzhu grinned at Maisie and Felix. "That would be cabbage cooked in bean oil and rice seasoned with mustard seed."

Felix gave his new friend a weak smile. Cabbage was slimy, and he never, ever put mustard on anything, even hot dogs.

"You children all need to wash your hands first," Zhenzhu's mother said. "And for goodness' sake, take that hat of yours off inside."

Zhenzhu grumbled but reached up and removed the red hat with gold Buddhas.

Both Maisie and Felix stared in disbelief as long, blond hair tumbled down Zhenzhu's shoulders.

"Pearl," Zhenzhu's mother said. "Show your friends to the sink."

Zhenzhu, they realized, was a girl.

·CHAPTER FIVE·

Pearl Buck

In the morning, the little house did not look as wonderful as it had in the dark. The bricks, Maisie saw now, were faded and chipped, and the little front porch sagged. Even the silk curtains and straw rugs did little to hide the condition of Pearl Sydenstricker's home. She looked down at the blue cotton trousers and tunic Mrs. Sydenstricker had given her. The fabric was slightly worn and frayed at the edges. Felix's was, too, Maisie noticed.

Felix nudged Maisie and tilted his chin toward a corner of the small room where they'd slept on a futon on the floor.

She had resolved to continue to ignore him, maybe forever. Hadn't Great-Aunt Maisie and

Uncle Thorne done just fine without each other all these years? But she sneaked a glance at what he was trying to show her. The biggest bugs she had ever seen slithered across the floor. They must have been eight inches long, with hard shells and lots of yellow legs.

Maisie let out a small yelp.

"*Zên me yàng?*" someone called to them.

A small, old woman appeared in the doorway. Her face was as wrinkled as a prune, and her hair was so thin that her leathery scalp showed through.

"*Zên me yàng?*" the woman repeated, and now Maisie saw that she was toothless as well.

Felix pointed to the bugs scurrying around.

The old woman tottered into the room laughing.

Maisie and Felix couldn't help but stare. Her feet in their faded cloth shoes were smaller than those insects. From beneath thick, white stockings, her three-inch-long feet moved in quick, mincing steps. How could she possibly walk on such tiny feet? They watched as she picked up an old slipper, which seemed to be there just for this purpose, and began smashing the bugs. A sickening crunch echoed every time she got one.

The old woman grinned her toothless grin at Maisie and Felix, threw the slipper down, and teetered out of the room.

"Her feet," Felix whispered.

But Maisie thrust her chin upward and did not answer.

"Please," Felix said. "Don't do this."

Maisie walked right out of the room without saying a word.

Pearl was in the kitchen with the old woman and a young Chinese girl holding a fat baby. All of them were eating rice from small bowls and laughing as the old woman talked.

When Pearl saw Maisie, she said, "You don't like our centipedes, I hear."

"Is that what they are?" Maisie said, grimacing.

"They're better than the scorpions," Pearl said.

Maisie swallowed hard. "Scorpions?"

"Mother hates them, too," Pearl said. "But Wang Amah came to your defense."

At the sound of her name, the old woman bowed slightly toward Pearl.

"She's my nurse," Pearl explained. "I love her mightily. And this is my *mèi mei*, Precious Cloud."

When she saw Maisie's look of confusion she added, "*Mèi mei.* Little sister."

Pearl lowered her voice. "Her mother died, so

she's come to live with us."

"Nice to meet you," Maisie said to Precious Cloud.

"Oh, she doesn't speak any English at all," Pearl said. "That baby she's holding is my little sister Grace. I think you've met all of us now."

Wang Amah held out a bowl of rice to Maisie. With chopsticks, she added something bright pink, chopped small scallions, and thin slivers of that white, lacy vegetable Maisie had seen in the marketplace.

"What is this?" Maisie asked.

"Pickled vegetables," Pearl told her. "And lotus root."

"Lotus root," Maisie said to herself. It sounded exotic, and she said again, softly this time, "Lotus root."

By now Felix had come into the kitchen, too, and Pearl made the introductions all over again.

"Nice to meet you," Felix said.

Precious Cloud stared at him blankly, but Wang Amah grinned her toothless grin at him and handed him a white porcelain bowl rimmed in red. Felix could smell something vinegary wafting up from it, and his stomach did a small flip. Last night, he had choked down the slimy cabbage. He had to be polite, and he was hungry.

All the while, though, he'd thought of the dan dan noodles from Szechuan Gourmet in New York and all the other Chinese food they used to get delivered to Bethune Street. This tasted nothing like that.

Maisie was happily scooping the rice and vegetables in her bowl into her mouth, just like she'd done with that dreadful cabbage last night.

Felix took a deep breath, then picked up the chopsticks in front of him and ate a small bit of rice. Not bad, he decided. He poked around at the vegetables, trying to determine what they were.

"Onion," Pearl said, pointing one of her own chopsticks at something in his bowl. "String bean. Bok choy. Lotus root."

He smiled at her gratefully.

As he ate the rice and vegetables, Felix tried not to stare too hard at Precious Cloud. She was beautiful, he thought. And familiar looking as if he'd met her before. He took a longer peek at Precious Cloud and smiled. She looked very much like Lily Goldberg, he realized. For an instant, he remembered Lily standing there in The Treasure Chest. Was she still standing there? He knew that when they time traveled, it was as if no time passed at home. But was it really no time at all? Would they return right where they'd left off to find Lily waiting?

"Pearl," Maisie was saying, "why do you wear your hair up in your hat like that? We thought you were a boy!"

Pearl laughed. "I never thought about that," she said. "Blond hair is considered worse than an animal's hair here. So Wang Amah always makes me hide it when I go out. You should, too, Maisie."

Maisie loved the idea. It felt mysterious and special to take her long hair and tuck it inside a cap like Pearl's, like a disguise.

"Okay," Maisie agreed. "I will."

Pearl stood. "Let's go sit on the veranda," she said. "We can see the river from there, and it's lovely to watch the boats in the morning."

"Like at home," Felix said. "In Newport where we live, I like to go to the wharf and look at all the sailboats."

"I like to imagine I can escape on one of them," Maisie said.

"Escape?" Pearl repeated.

"I don't like Newport. Not one bit."

Pearl nodded sympathetically. "My mother doesn't like China very much," she said. "But honestly, I can't imagine living anywhere else."

Wang Amah followed them out to the porch. Maisie saw that it wasn't a front porch as it had seemed last night, but instead wrapped around the little house. From it, they could indeed see the Yangtze River with its junks and sampans moving along it. A fine mist hung over the river and the hills. Everyone settled into rattan chairs that faced the river.

"What are those sticks coming out of the river?" Felix asked.

"That's bamboo," Pearl said.

On a hill in the distance they could just make out the outline of a slender building with a gently sloping, pointed roof.

"What's that building?" Maisie said, pointing to it.

"That's a pagoda," Pearl said.

Maisie nodded happily. A pagoda. She'd heard the word before, of course. But now here she was, sitting in China and looking at a real one on a hill above the Yangtze River. A shiver of excitement ran through her.

Wang Amah began to speak in Chinese.

"She says that there's a dragon in that pagoda," Pearl translated. "He's kept underneath it. If he gets free, he'll flood the river and drown us all."

"A dragon?" Felix said.

"There aren't any dragons," Maisie said dismissively.

"Wang Amah believes these stories," Pearl said.

With her long, blond hair and bright-blue eyes, Maisie would have thought Pearl seemed out of place here. Yet she was obviously so connected to China and her home that Pearl Sydenstricker seemed as Chinese as Wang Amah and Precious Cloud did.

"According to Chinese beliefs," Pearl explained, "there are storm dragons and sea dragons and all kinds of demons and spirits. They live all around us. In the clouds and the trees. Even in the rocks."

"That's—" Maisie began.

"Romantic," Felix interrupted. He loved stories of all kinds. And he didn't want his sister to be rude.

Wang Amah began to talk again, Pearl nodding as she listened.

"She's telling us about daggers that are magical," Pearl said when the old woman had finished. "A man can make them very small and hide them in his ear or in the corner of his eye. But if a demon attacks him, he can take the dagger out, and it will grow large and fast and sharp enough to slay it."

Pearl sighed contentedly. Obviously she loved the myths that Wang Amah told her.

"I don't care for fairy tales," Maisie said.

"I like them," Felix said. He looked out at the mist. It was easy to imagine dragons and spirits out there among the bamboo and green hills.

Pearl leaned toward Maisie. "Wang Amah's real life is even more exciting than her fairy tales."

She spoke in rapid Chinese to Wang Amah, who smiled her toothless smile and began once again to talk. This time Pearl didn't wait for her to finish the whole story. Instead, she translated as the old woman spoke, their two voices creating a harmony of words.

"I was once very beautiful. My skin was not always brown and wrinkled like it is now. Rather, it was as white as the clouds. And my hair was as black as the night. I wore it in one long, thick braid that fell down my back to my knees. This was in Yangzhou, far from here. My father was prosperous, and he married me off when I was very young to protect me from the soldiers who preyed on young women."

Wang Amah sighed. "That is how lovely I was."

She paused as if remembering, and then began again.

"But then came the rebellion that swept China. They say millions were killed. Maybe as many as ten or twenty million. This I don't know

for certain. But I do know that everyone I loved
died then. Mother. Father. Husband. I only
survived because I hid in a well. When I emerged,
our pagoda was on fire with all the monks
trapped inside."

"You mean they all burned to death?" Felix
said in horror.

Pearl sighed. "Wang Amah's life could be a
novel, don't you think?"

Glancing at the old woman's feet, Maisie
whispered, "What happened to her feet?" She
imagined the soldiers slicing them with bayonets
or Wang Amah running into that burning
pagoda to save the monks.

"They're bound, of course," Pearl said,
surprised.

"Like, tied up?" Felix asked. Even though
he didn't like to look at those tiny feet inside the
small, cloth shoes, he peeked at them.

"No, no," Pearl said, shaking her head. "The
Chinese bind their daughters' feet when they're
very young. Wang Amah was only three when her
parents did hers."

"But why did they do that?" Maisie asked.
Unlike Felix, she couldn't stop looking at those
tiny feet.

"The goal is to stop the feet from growing,"

Pearl explained. "At first, they break the four small toes and force them under the sole. That's to make them narrow and shorter. Then they wrap them in bandages really, really tightly, and every day they tighten them even more. The whole thing takes about two years."

Felix looked at Wang Amah's kind, old face and thought about all she had endured.

"But why do they do it?" Maisie asked again.

"I've heard several stories," Pearl said. "But I like the one that says it began so that women could walk like Princess Yao Niang. It's said that she walked so gracefully it was as if she skimmed over the top of golden lilies. Every woman in China wanted to be a lily-footed woman."

"I think it's barbaric!" Felix blurted.

But Pearl just shrugged. "It's the custom here. My friends' mothers do it to them."

"It sounds terrible," Maisie said. "Painful."

"Amah says that her parents made her sleep alone in the outhouse so they wouldn't have to hear her cries of pain all night."

Pearl brightened. "Do you want to see them?"

"No!" Felix said, just as Maisie said, "Yes!"

Amah and Pearl spoke in Chinese for several minutes. Then the old woman bent and removed her small shoes and white stockings.

As she began to unwrap the bandages, Felix got up, panicked. "I don't want to see deformed feet," he said.

"In China," Pearl said gently, putting a hand on his arm, "they are considered beautiful. And Amah's, at only three inches long, are the ideal golden lilies."

"There are so many bandages," Maisie said, watching Amah unroll them.

"She has to wear them all the time, even when she sleeps," Pearl explained.

Finally, the last of the bandages came off, and Wang Amah lifted her tiny foot for them to see.

Felix pretended to look, but as soon as he caught a glimpse of the deformed lump, he averted his gaze. Maisie, however, gawked. The skin was black and purple, and the foot itself had been reduced to just the big toe. But on closer inspection, she saw that the other four toes were indeed fused below the arch.

"*Xie xie.*" Pearl softly thanked Amah.

The old woman slowly began the process of putting the bandages back on. As she did, she said something to Pearl.

"Amah says every pair of small feet costs a bath of tears," Pearl translated.

Wang Amah spoke again to Pearl.

"She wants to take us to Horse Street," Pearl told Maisie and Felix. "Where I met you yesterday," she added.

"Is it okay with your mother?" Felix asked.

"Sure. She needs to stay here and take care of Grace," Pearl said. "Do you want to go to Horse Street then?"

"All right," Maisie said eagerly.

With each passing hour, Maisie became more and more enchanted by China, with its bamboo rising from the river in the mist, the storybook pagoda, and green rice paddies. She loved the smells in the air, the gardenias and roses mixing with spices from the kitchen. She even loved Wang Amah's stories, with their soldiers and burning monks and foot bindings.

Felix recognized the look that had spread over his sister's face. Once again, she would want to stay in the past instead of going home to Newport and their mother. This happened every time. The simple life on Clara Barton's farm and the return with Alexander Hamilton to New York— even the New York of the eighteenth century— appealed to her much more than their own new life. Certain that they would give the jade box to Pearl and the time would come for them to leave, he could already foresee the arguments they would have when Maisie refused to try to get back. Felix sighed.

"Are you all right?" Pearl asked him.

"He's fine," Maisie said knowingly.

Pearl threw her arm around Felix's shoulder. "Just wait," she said. "Amah always buys the candy Mother forbids me from having. You'll love it."

Once again, Felix tried to meet Maisie's eyes. And once again, Maisie ignored him completely.

· CHAPTER SIX ·

The Year of the Rat

Telling stories marked the days with Pearl. Wang Amah, Mrs. Sydenstricker, and even Pearl herself were all masterful storytellers. Maisie and Felix loved to sit out on the veranda in the morning and hear their stories about life in China and Chinese legends and myths. At night, Felix wrote down the stories he'd heard to take back to Lily Goldberg, who so desperately longed for information about her culture.

They spent a lot of time in the kitchen, too, where Chushi, the cook, fed them salted fish, pickled vegetables, tofu, and—to Felix's surprise, his favorite—the crunchy rice from the bottom of the pan. Never before had he liked anything crunchy, but this rice changed his mind about crunchy food. Chushi told them stories, too. He loved to read, and every day he would act out parts he'd read the night before from Chinese novels. Tall, with a thin, long face and graceful hands, he imitated birds flying and oceans rolling.

Pearl translated, and Maisie and Felix sat, transfixed, eating and listening.

The story Pearl asked Chushi to tell again and again was "The Dream of the Red Chamber," a kind of Chinese Romeo and Juliet story about star-crossed lovers from warring tribes.

"Ah," Chushi always said, shaking his head, "you are a romantic, Zhenzhu."

土　土　土　土　土

In the afternoon, the children often went to Horse Street. Wang Amah gave Maisie a hat like Pearl's and tucked her mop of hair beneath it, muttering in Chinese as she did.

"Don't eat that candy," Pearl's mother always ordered as they left the house.

Mrs. Sydenstricker seemed to have an unusually strong obsession with germs. Every day she washed the walls and floors of the house with a strong-smelling chemical. She fretted over Pearl and baby Grace, feeling their foreheads for fevers, listening to their chests, and watching them closely as if they might disappear.

One day as they ate the forbidden candy from its paper cones, Maisie asked Pearl why her mother didn't want her to eat it. The candy was just crystallized sugar, like the rock candy Maisie and Felix liked to get at the little candy store in Cape May when their family went on vacation.

"She thinks it's dirty," Pearl said with a shrug.

Felix forced himself to swallow what was already in his mouth.

"Dirty?" he asked.

"She thinks everything in China is dirty," Pearl said sadly. "My father doesn't. If he were home more, I wouldn't have to sneak like this."

So far, Felix and Maisie hadn't even met Pearl's father. He was too busy trying to convert people up north to bother coming home for a visit.

"She worries about you a lot," Felix said.

Pearl hesitated before she answered. "My father says we've had a cup full of sorrow. My sisters Maude and Edith and my brother Arthur, all of them older than me, went away too soon."

When she saw the puzzled looks on Maisie's and Felix's faces, she added, "They died."

"Died!" Maisie said, shocked.

"As did my brother Clyde," Pearl said sadly.

"But how?" Maisie managed to ask.

"Mother blames China. The summer heat, the lack of hospitals."

Felix blinked back tears. Four children? All dead? No wonder Pearl's mother was such a worrier. For the first time since they'd arrived in China last week, when Felix looked at Maisie, she returned his glance.

"You can't die from the heat, though, can you?" Felix said. As a worrier himself, and a bit of a hypochondriac, the idea that heat could actually kill you started a panic in his chest.

"Well," Pearl said. "They died from diseases."

Felix swallowed hard. The taste of the candy had turned sour in his mouth.

"Diphtheria, cholera, malaria . . ."

To Maisie, these sounded like diseases from novels, terrible but unreal.

Felix wondered if his vaccinations would hold up here. Every year when their mother took them to the pediatrician, there always seemed to be another booster shot waiting. Were any of them for cholera?

"Poor angels," Pearl said.

Later that afternoon, when Pearl took her daily turn of rocking Grace on the veranda and

Mrs. Sydenstricker joined them there, Felix understood the sadness that marked her face.

Still, as she sewed a ruffle on the bottom of new curtains, when Pearl begged her, Mrs. Sydenstricker readily agreed to tell them her story about how she saved her home and children from a gang of men who believed Westerners' presence in the valley had brought on the drought.

"This was in August," Mrs. Sydenstricker began, "ten years ago. We went so long without rain that the rice withered in the fields. Absalom—Mr. Sydenstricker—was away from home as usual, when the men appeared beneath our window with knives and clubs. I heard them discussing how to break in and kill every last one of us."

Felix gasped. His eyes drifted to the fields beyond the house as if he might be able to see bandits waiting there, too.

"The night was so hot," Mrs. Sydenstricker continued, "that perspiration dripped down my forehead into my eyes and the children's nightclothes grew wet."

She paused for a moment, and her eyes got a faraway look. Felix wondered if she was remembering those four children she'd lost.

But then Mrs. Sydenstricker grew animated again. "The air was still and thick. The closest

Americans who could help were almost a hundred miles away, and the mob was ready to enter."

"Tell us what you did, Mother," Pearl said excitedly, even though she knew the story well.

"I picked up my broom and swept the floor clean."

"You cleaned the house while right outside the door men were planning to murder your family?" Maisie asked.

"That's right. And then I mixed the batter for my best vanilla cake, and I put it in the oven to bake. I set the table with our best teacups and plates and lit the lamps and waited for my guests to arrive," Mrs. Sydenstricker said.

"Guests!" Felix said, staring at Mrs. Sydenstricker as if he had never seen her before. Right before his eyes she was transforming from a sad and anxious mother into a superhero.

"Weren't you terrified?" Maisie asked.

"Yes," she admitted.

Pearl was beaming up at her mother proudly. "So when the men broke down the door—"

"When the men finally broke down our front door, they found me playing with my children and ready for a tea party." Mrs. Sydenstricker laughed. "Well, they didn't know what to make of this scene. The meanest one of all, the leader, accepted the cup of tea I offered him and then motioned for the others to do the same. We all had tea and my delicious cake, and then they left."

"They left?" Maisie said. She, too, was seeing Pearl's mother as someone completely different.

"You are so brave!" Felix blurted.

"I was trembling, Felix. Trembling the entire time," Mrs. Sydenstricker said. "I think I trembled for a week afterward."

"And then what?" Pearl asked.

"And then, like magic, the rain came that very night."

土　　土　　土　　土　　土

Maisie and Felix fell into the rhythms of these days easily. Slowly, Maisie's anger at her brother began to melt away. For the first time in their travels, neither of them felt the urge, or the panic, to get back home. There were days when Maisie thought she could live here forever, listening to Wang Amah and Mrs. Sydenstricker and the cook telling stories, sitting on the veranda watching the boats on the Yangtze River.

When homesickness struck Felix, he calmed himself by remembering that no matter how long they stayed, when they returned home they would still be at the VIP Christmas party and Lily Goldberg would be standing right there in The

Treasure Chest where they'd left her. Felix had that small, jade box in his pocket. Sometimes at night, he opened its lid and touched the dark dirt inside, wondering why regular dirt would ever matter to Pearl. He knew that someday he would know when to give it to Pearl. And that was when it would be time to go home. But for now, except for occasional pangs of missing his own mother and their apartment in Elm Medona, he, too, was happy. He liked to play with the paper lanterns shaped like animals that they bought on Horse Street and to sit in the warm kitchen with everyone, and of course, hear their stories.

Days passed in this way. And then weeks.

Walking together down Horse Street one afternoon, Maisie said, "Felix, do you think that no matter how long we stay here, when we go back no time will have passed?"

"Ye-es," Felix said thoughtfully. *What is my sister trying to do now?* he wondered miserably.

"Then why go back?" Maisie asked. "I mean, we could stay here until we get older and still be able to pick up right where we left off at the Christmas party, right?"

"I don't know," Felix said. "And I don't care because we aren't going to stay here for years and years."

The noise and action and smells on Horse Street—the vendors and the letter writers and the men cooking in the woks—all felt familiar to Maisie and Felix now. And this familiarity combined with what Maisie was saying made Felix's chest tighten. He didn't want to grow up here. He wanted to be back in Anne Hutchinson Elementary School with Jim Duncan and Lily Goldberg and Miss Landers.

"But why not?" Maisie said.

They had reached the man who sold the candy in paper cones, and Maisie rooted around in her pockets for a coin to buy some.

"Don't, Maisie," Felix said.

She looked at him, surprised.

"Maybe Mrs. Sydenstricker is right and we shouldn't eat it. Maybe it's full of . . . I don't know . . . cholera or something."

Maisie found a coin and dropped it in the candy man's hand. "Don't be silly," she said, taking a bite of candy. "Nothing bad is going to happen to us."

"You don't know that!" Felix said. "What if you got one of those diseases that killed Pearl's sisters and brothers?"

Maisie chewed her candy, considering. "I guess you're right," she said finally.

Felix sighed. "Maisie, as much as you don't like it, we have a life back in Newport."

"And we have one here now, too," she said.

They continued down Horse Street in silence. Maybe it was time to give Pearl the jade box, Felix thought. Maybe it was time to go home.

土　土　土　土　土

"Rat years," Mr. Kung, their tutor, said solemnly, "are associated with wealth." The tutor came to visit Pearl, Felix, and Maisie a few times a week.

He paused and let his watery eyes alight on first Pearl's face, then Maisie's, and then Felix's.

"But," he continued, "it is also associated with death."

Felix shivered in his dark-blue cotton tunic. They all stood on top of a green hill that ran behind Pearl's house. Mr. Kung held a giant, red kite shaped like a fish with golden scales. The wind rippled the fish's head slightly, making it look as if it were shaking its head at them.

"The rat," Mr. Kung added in his serious, deep voice, "is the first animal in the twelve-year cycle because it sneakily rode on the back of the ox and jumped off near the finishing line. This story shows us its attributes." As he said each one, he held up a finger, counting them. "Cunning. Aggression. Leadership. Hard work. Strong will."

All five fingers of one hand stood up.

"But what will this year bring? Year 4598?"

Maisie didn't mind the idea that the Year of the Rat brought wealth. But death? She didn't like that at all. Luckily, she decided, she didn't believe in Chinese astrology or myths or anything. Mr. Kung was just creepy.

He had arrived this morning with *nian gao*, rice cakes made from sticky rice, sugar, chestnuts, dates, and lotus leaves. "In Chinese," Mr. Kung had explained, "*nian gao* sounds the same as the saying for getting higher year by year. In Chinese people's minds, the higher you are, the more prosperous your business is. Very fortuitous to eat *nian gao* on New Year's."

That morning, as Chushi and Wang Amah worked on all the specialties they would have for dinner tonight, Mr. Kung explained the significance of each one.

"Ah, very good," he said, pointing to the fish the cook was filleting. "In Chinese, fish sounds like 'save more.' Chinese people always like to save more money at the end of the year because they think if they save more, they can make more in the next year. So we eat fish to remind us to save more."

Then he peered closely at Wang Amah's dumplings, which were all stuffed and crimped, waiting on a bamboo platter to be fried.

"Dumplings have a long history in China," he said, nodding his approval at Wang Amah's perfect crescent shapes. "More than eighteen hundred years. To me, they symbolize Chinese food. The more dumplings you eat during the New Year celebration, the more money you can make in the New Year."

Wang Amah had started to fill spring roll wrappers with a vegetable mixture, then roll them into tight, cigar-shaped cylinders.

Mr. Kung nodded approvingly. "When she fries these, they will turn a beautiful gold. The gold of money. The gold of spring." He grinned at them, revealing a set of long, yellow teeth.

"Gold like his teeth," Maisie whispered to Felix.

Since she had just stopped ignoring him, Felix smiled, even though he kind of liked Mr. Kung. All the information he gave them was interesting, Felix thought. Plus, when they got home, he would dazzle Lily Goldberg with everything he knew about China.

Now, out on the hill with the kite, Mr. Kung turned his solemn eyes on the three of them.

"This kite will predict what will happen in this Year of the Rat," he told them.

"How can a kite do that?" Maisie said in her demanding voice.

Felix cringed. But Mr. Kung remained unfazed.

"We let the wind tell us," Mr. Kung answered mysteriously.

Maisie rolled her eyes.

"Do you know how to fly a kite, Zhenzhu?" he asked Pearl. Even though he spoke English, Mr. Kung always used Pearl's Chinese name.

She shook her head.

"Very simple," Mr. Kung said.

Carefully, he placed the kite in both of Pearl's hands.

"Hold it like so," he instructed.

Mr. Kung stared off beyond the hills. He licked one finger and held it up into the air, nodding.

"There is a good amount of wind to fly a kite today," he said, pleased. "All you must do is toss the kite lightly up into the wind, and the wind will do the rest."

"Just throw it?" Pearl said hesitantly.

Mr. Kung considered this. "No," he said. "Toss. Lightly."

Pearl nodded.

Mr. Kung placed a hand on her arm.

"Zhenzhu," he said, "when the wind lifts the kite, you must let it go so that it can fly toward heaven and forecast the future."

"What?" Maisie said. "The kite is going to forecast the future?" She shook her head. Mr. Kung might be a good teacher, but his beliefs in superstitions were silly.

"On the New Year, this is what we do," he said, looking directly at Maisie. "It is the Chinese way."

Maisie and Felix watched as Pearl took a few running steps across the grass, then lifted the kite upward and let it go.

The kite seemed to hang there for an instant as if it were deciding what to do. Then it dipped dangerously low to the ground.

Pearl ran to retrieve it, but Mr. Kung held her back.

A gust of wind came from nowhere, and it lifted the kite high, then higher still.

They all gazed upward at the bright-red kite against the light-blue sky. The sun made the gold scales shimmer, and briefly the kite actually looked like a fish swimming. Felix wondered what it meant for the future that the kite was going so high. Nothing bad, he decided. It must be a good sign.

But just as suddenly as it lifted, the kite took a

nosedive and came crashing toward the ground. *Oh no*, Felix thought as he watched it. The word *death* echoed in his mind.

Right before it hit, the kite hovered, then slowly lifted upward once again.

They watched as it drifted skyward.

"What does it mean?" Pearl asked, still watching the kite float.

"This year," Mr. Kung said, "will be a year of ups and downs."

He glanced toward the sky and the distant speck of kite disappearing.

"But all will be well," he said unconvincingly.

Still gazing upward, Mr. Kung nodded to himself.

"Yes," he said. "All will be well in the end."

Felix wished he believed him.

·CHAPTER SEVEN·

The Boxer Rebellion

On a beautiful, sunny spring morning, Mr. Kung sat with Maisie, Felix, and Pearl on a grassy hill overlooking the river. They were practicing their calligraphy, writing the beautiful and complicated Chinese characters in thick, dark ink.

Whenever one of them made a sloppy or imprecise character, Mr. Kung made them do it all over again.

"When letters were invented," he reminded them each time, "heaven rejoiced. They must be written with reverence."

Felix carefully practiced the characters for *family* and *friend* so that he could teach Lily how to make them when he got back home. *Home.* As time passed, Felix was getting more homesick. When he counted up the days and then weeks and months since they'd been here and realized it had been six months since they landed in the market, he grew worried that they weren't going to be able to get back. The Christmas party and Lily Goldberg seemed almost blurry to him now. Still, Maisie reminded him often—too often—that they had stayed away a long time last time, too, and they'd gotten back easily.

Maisie's letters were always sloppier than Felix's, and she and Mr. Kung argued over his insistence that she practice until she get them just right.

"Maisie," Mr. Kung said, exasperated, "he who does not show reverence to lettered paper is no better than a blind buffalo."

"Says who?" Maisie demanded, putting her pen down.

"Says Confucius," Mr. Kung told her.

Even Maisie didn't argue with Confucius. She dipped her pen in ink again and tried to make the strokes as neatly as she could.

On their way back home, Maisie stopped and pointed to a tree with small boxes hanging from its limbs.

"What are those?" she asked Mr. Kung.

"Ah!" he said. "Inside those boxes are papers,

letters, anything with writing on it. You see, Maisie, writing is so powerful that the only way to dispose of it properly is to burn it in those boxes, then hang it on a tree so that the smoke takes it back to heaven where it belongs."

Maisie studied the tree, thinking hard.

"I like it, Mr. Kung," she said finally. "I'll try harder tomorrow."

"You are a smart girl," Mr. Kung said, patting her back.

They arrived back home in good moods.

"I'm sure Wang Amah saved you some crunchy rice, Felix," Pearl said.

But her mother met them at the door, frowning.

"Your father is home," she said. She glanced at Mr. Kung, whose smile had turned to a worried expression.

Absalom Sydenstricker, Pearl's father, had only come home one other time since Maisie and Felix had been with the family. His fierce expression and the large stick he carried everywhere with him made Maisie and Felix afraid to be around him. Even worse, he spoke in a loud, booming voice about how the Chinese were heathens and he meant to convert every last one of them. Pearl told them that so far he'd only managed to convert about a dozen. But he refused to give up.

After he left and went back up north, the whole house seemed to sigh with relief. Pearl told Maisie and Felix that he did not even mourn all the children he and her mother had lost. "He believes it's selfish to cry for yourself when there's an entire nation of heathens to cry for."

Now he was back.

"Is he all right?" Mr. Kung asked.

Mrs. Sydenstricker glanced at Pearl, then shook her head.

"He had to close down chapels," she added. "The landlords refused to rent to him because he's a foreigner."

"What's going on?" Maisie asked.

"The Boxers," Mrs. Sydenstricker said.

"Mother, you know that's not what they call themselves. They're the Righteous Fists of Harmony," Pearl said. "Only foreigners call them the Boxers."

Pearl's mother looked at her. "Darling, we *are* foreigners. And your father reports that they are even more committed to ridding China of us." She hesitated and then said, "They gave him a pretty bad beating. He has bruises everywhere."

"This is very worrisome," Mr. Kung said quietly.

Wang Amah came into the living room, wringing her hands. She said something in Chinese, and Pearl translated.

"Amah says that they believe Westerners are responsible for the famine and floods that have struck parts of China. They blame Westerners for all of China's problems."

Pearl's mother said sadly, "Precious Cloud has gone to stay with a Chinese family. She doesn't think it's safe to stay with us anymore."

"No!" Pearl cried.

Heavy footsteps pounded down the stairs, and Mr. Sydenstricker appeared in the doorway. His very presence silenced Pearl and all of them.

"It's official," he announced. "The empress has officially asked the Boxers to rid China of all foreigners."

"She always gets what she wants," Mrs. Sydenstricker said. She looked at her husband. "We must leave. We must take the children to safety at once."

"Nonsense!" Mr. Sydenstricker said in his booming preacher voice. "We must face the heathens head-on!"

Mrs. Sydenstricker's jaw muscles tightened and released as she stared at her husband in disbelief. Then, without a word, she turned and ran out of the room and up the stairs. The sound of her sobbing filled the house for the rest of the day and long into the night.

"Maybe we should give her the box and go home," Felix whispered to Maisie in the dark.

"We survived a fire at sea with Alexander Hamilton," Maisie reminded him. "Nothing bad will happen to us if we stay."

"I like it here, too," Felix said softly. "But it sounds like it's getting dangerous for foreigners."

Maisie didn't answer. Felix sighed. He knew that the time would come for them to leave China and Pearl behind, and he knew that Maisie would resist.

"Remember," Maisie said, "Pearl Sydenstricker is probably going to grow up and do something wonderful. She isn't going to get killed by these Boxers."

Now it was Felix who didn't answer. Instead, he reached for his sister's hand and took it in his own. They slept that way all night, holding hands, each of them dreaming their different dreams.

First, Mr. Kung stopped coming.

Then, foreigners from the north began arriving in Zhenjiang. Their clothes were ripped, their bodies bruised and broken. They told stories of the Boxers beating them and burning their houses. Frightened, they arranged for junks to take them to Shanghai for safety. Many of them told stories of how their children had starved to death or died from sickness along the way. With each new story Mrs. Sydenstricker heard, she begged her husband to let them leave. Each time, he refused. More resolved than ever, he insisted he must stay and fight the heathens.

Still, Mrs. Sydenstricker had Pearl, Maisie, and Felix fold all their clothes and leave them on a chair by their beds. "In case we have to leave quickly in the night," she told them.

Maisie and Felix wore the cotton pants, tunics, and cloth shoes that all the children wore. They folded them neatly along with the party clothes they'd arrived in. At night, they lay in bed, Felix trembling with fear and Maisie trembling with excitement. The sound of Pearl's parents arguing rang throughout the house.

土　土　土　土　土

On the day the empress issued an imperial edict calling for death to all foreigners, Maisie and Felix sneaked out of the house and walked to Horse Street. They did this every afternoon while Mrs. Sydenstricker napped and Pearl rocked baby Grace on the veranda. Both of them hid their hair under hats just like Pearl did whenever they went out.

"I think it's time," Felix said. "I'm really afraid of what these Boxers might do next."

Maisie didn't answer.

Out of habit, Felix reached into his pocket to touch the little jade box.

"Oh no!" he said. "The box is missing!"

He stopped walking and looked around the ground. "We have to retrace our steps," he said. "Without that box, we'll never get home."

Panicked, he began to walk back in the direction from which they'd come, his eyes desperately on the lookout for the box. What if the dirt spilled when the box fell from his pocket? Felix wondered. Was the dirt important, too?

He turned to ask Maisie these very questions, but she was nowhere to be found.

"Maisie!" he called.

At first he heard nothing. Then a loud scream came from down the road.

Felix stood, frozen for a moment, until his sister's voice cut through the silence.

"Felix! Felix! Help!"

In an instant, Felix was running back toward Horse Street, his heart pounding so hard he thought it might break through his ribs. He opened his mouth to tell her he was coming, but his voice came out like a squeak.

"Help! Help!" Maisie yelled.

Right before the marketplace, Horse Street split and part of it dipped down toward the river. Felix followed Maisie's voice there, tripping over roots that stuck out of the ground and scraping his arms on low branches as he ran.

On the bank of the river, a small group of teenagers stood huddled together. And in the middle of them, crouched and covering her face with her hands, was Maisie. Her hat had come off, and all Felix could see clearly was her mop of hair. What were these boys doing? he wondered as he ran, panting.

"Hey!" he called to them, his voice finally returning.

A few of the teenagers turned in his direction. Felix saw then that they had big sticks in their hands. One of them held a large rock in the air, about to bring it down on Maisie.

Felix increased his speed and leaped at the boy with the rock, knocking him to the ground and landing on top of him with a big thud.

The boys with the sticks poked him hard in the ribs, taunting him in Chinese as they did. Felix tried to ward them off, but he couldn't. The boy beneath him threw Felix off of him. Now Felix was flat on his back looking up into a crowd of angry faces.

The biggest, meanest boy of them all took a step closer to Felix, his stick raised high.

Felix closed his eyes tight, preparing for the terrible blow.

"*Zǔ zhǐ!*" someone shouted. "*Zǔ zhǐ!*"

Felix peeked from beneath his eyelids and saw the boys scattering.

"*Zǔ zhǐ!*"

There, in the middle of them all, stood Wang Amah, slapping them on the arms and shooing them away.

Carefully, Felix sat up. His side stung from where he'd been poked. Now he could see Maisie clearly. Her cheek was scraped and bleeding, and her arms had red welts all over them.

Wang Amah helped Maisie to her feet, scolding them in rapid Chinese.

Felix's and Maisie's eyes met above Wang Amah's head.

"I have it," Maisie said through her tears.

"Have what?" Felix said.

"The box. I took it so we couldn't leave."

Even though he wanted to be angry with her, the sight of his strong, independent sister hurt and crying made Felix rush to her side and throw his arms around her.

"I don't care," he said, hugging her.

Maisie reached into her own pocket and pulled out the jade box.

"Here," she said. "I think it's time we gave this to Pearl."

⼟   ⼟   ⼟   ⼟   ⼟

The next morning, Maisie and Felix woke up and headed to the kitchen as usual. Mrs. Sydenstricker had been so angry at them for sneaking out that they'd gone to bed early to avoid her. Even as she gently cleaned Maisie's cuts, she'd shook her head in disappointment.

"I hope we're not still in trouble," Maisie said.

"I hope Mr. Sydenstricker doesn't yell at us. He scares me even when I'm not in trouble."

To their surprise, the atmosphere in the kitchen was light, like it had been before all the trouble with the Boxers, before Mr. Sydenstricker had returned home to stay. Wang Amah and Chushi were chattering happily, and Pearl sat eating rice and salted fish out of her bowl with chopsticks.

"Father has gone to give communion to an old lady," Pearl said.

That explained the lighter mood, Felix realized. Without the frightening presence of Pearl's father, everyone relaxed.

The day took on the old rhythms. Chushi told

them the story of the Red Dragon, acting out each part. After breakfast, they all sat on the veranda, and Wang Amah told them once more about her childhood and her daring escape from the soldiers.

"I wish we could go to Horse Street and get some candy," Pearl said. "That would make today perfect."

But Wang Amah would not hear of it. "Danger!" she shouted in Chinese. "Danger!"

Relieved, Felix went with Pearl to the hills behind the house to fly a kite. Even Maisie didn't want to leave and stayed behind instead to rock Grace on the porch.

The wind wasn't very strong, and neither of them could get the kite into the air. Finally they gave up and flopped onto the warm grass.

"Felix?" Pearl said. "Aren't your parents worried about you?"

His mind drifted to the Christmas party. "I don't think so," he answered honestly.

"Are you orphans?" Pearl asked gently.

Felix didn't know how to answer. As he struggled for a reply, Pearl said, "It's okay. You don't need to be embarrassed."

Felix propped himself up on one elbow.

"I have something for you," he said. "A thank-you present for letting us stay with your family."

"Is it candy?" Pearl said, her eyes shining at the idea.

"No," Felix said. "Sorry."

He reached into his pocket and pulled out the jade box.

"Here," he said.

Pearl grinned. "It's pretty," she said. *"Xiè xie."*

"Bié kéqi," Felix said effortlessly. *You're welcome.*

"What should I keep in it?" Pearl asked, starting to lift the lid.

Felix grabbed her hand. "Oh," he said, "there's already something in there."

"A ring?" Pearl asked playfully. "A brooch?"

Felix shook his head. "I don't even know what a brooch is," he said.

"A pin," Pearl explained. "A fancy pin that ladies wear."

"No," he said. "Sorry. It's nothing like that."

Pearl opened the lid and frowned.

"Why did you fill it with dirt from our yard?" she asked, puzzled.

"How do you know that dirt is from here?" Felix asked her.

Pearl put some on her fingers and showed Felix.

"The color," she said. "The earth here has this color. I would recognize it anywhere."

Pearl laughed. "But I certainly don't need more of it," she said, pointing at the hills.

Without warning, she tipped the box to empty the dirt from it.

"No!" Felix shouted.

The dirt seemed to float in the air.

"Don't throw out the dirt," Felix said.

"You're so odd," Pearl said. "Why would I need to keep dirt?"

Felix swallowed hard. "Maybe," he began, then paused before continuing. "Maybe no matter where you go you'll always take this with you," he said. "Maybe it will inspire you someday."

Pearl studied Felix's face until he squirmed under her stare. "Maybe it will," she said finally.

土　土　土　土　土

Felix thought that Mrs. Sydenstricker was trying very hard not to look worried. But he could see how she jumped at every small noise and glanced out the window anxiously whenever she thought no one could see. Evening had arrived without any word from Mr. Sydenstricker. After dinner, Pearl tried to amuse everyone by making up stories, but her mother could not concentrate. Finally, she sent them all to bed.

"Do you think he's been killed?" Felix asked Maisie.

Remembering the gang on Horse Street, she shuddered.

"I thought an empress would be beautiful," Maisie said. "But Pearl told me she's old and wrinkled. Like Wang Amah."

"Wang Amah saved our lives," Felix said.

"I know."

"Maisie," Felix said. "I gave it to her."

"Gave what? To who?" Maisie asked, confused.

"The box. I gave it to Pearl this afternoon."

"Again?" Maisie said. "You went behind my back again?"

"I didn't go behind your back," Felix began. "You said yourself that it was time for us to give it to her."

"Us, Felix! Not you! Us!"

"I did it so we could get home if we needed to," Felix said. "I was trying to help us."

"First you take Lily Goldberg to The Treasure Chest, deliberately leaving me behind. And now—"

"Now I did exactly what you said to do."

He waited for Maisie's reply, but a moment of chilling silence passed.

"Maisie," he pleaded. "Come on."

But his sister just rolled away from him and kept her back turned the entire night.

Felix woke to the sound of excited shouts and racing footsteps. Maisie was already out of bed. As he dressed quickly, he remembered her harsh words the night before. Great-Aunt Maisie and her twin brother, Thorne, had never spoken again after a fight. Would his sister really do the same to him?

Everyone was standing in the doorway. The heat shimmered in the distance. Already the day was so hot that Felix started to sweat just walking from his room to the front door.

Pearl turned to him when she heard him approach. "Look!" she said. "Father is home safely!"

Sure enough, Mr. Sydenstricker was coming up the path to the house. As he neared, Felix saw blood on his cheek and forehead, but his blue eyes shone with joy.

At the threshold, he stopped and grinned.

"Lin Meng has been martyred!" he said victoriously. "Lin Meng has entered heaven!"

Mrs. Sydenstricker's hand went to her heart. "No," she said softly, shaking her head. "Oh no."

Her husband took her hands in his and smiled. "He is standing with the lord!" he said, his voice again filled with joy. "I saw it with my own eyes."

"Children," Mrs. Sydenstricker said, "go to the

kitchen with Amah and have your breakfast."

But none of them could move. Instead, they stood transfixed as they tried to make sense of the strangely joyful tone and the terrible story they told. Lin Meng, the son of the old woman he'd gone to give communion to, had been murdered? In front of Mr. Sydenstricker? Yet he was jubilant.

"The soldiers raided the house as I was administering communion. They tied me to a post." Here, he held his arms up in triumph to display the rope burns on his wrists. "And they tortured Lin Meng to death." Mr. Sydenstricker's voice filled with wonder. "My own convert," he said. "A martyr."

"Isn't a martyr someone who dies for their beliefs?" Maisie whispered to Pearl.

"He believes being a martyr is even better than being just a convert," Pearl whispered back.

"He thinks dying is a good thing?" Felix said, unable to keep his voice low.

"Absalom," Mrs. Sydenstricker said harshly. "You're frightening the children. I've had enough. I'm taking the children to Shanghai. Nothing will happen to these children. Do you hear me? Nothing."

Mr. Sydenstricker looked at her, surprised.

"I refuse to leave now. How could I? With the possibility of my own martyrdom so near?"

His wife gasped. "Absalom!" she said in disbelief.

"You have always put your own needs before the souls of the heathens here," he said sadly.

She studied her husband's face for a long time.

"Stay then," she said finally. "But you must hire a junk to wait for us on the river so that we can escape. I've already mapped out a route through the bamboo."

This time he studied her face.

"Fine," he said. "I will go now and make the arrangements. When the time is right, you will be able to leave."

Over the next few days, the heat worsened. The entire family stayed in the dark in the living room. It was so hot that Mr. Sydenstricker took off his preacher's white collar, the first time Maisie and Felix had seen him without it. Mrs. Sydenstricker entertained them with stories of the Civil War battles and the bravery of the Americans. Maisie understood these stories were meant to build their own courage and to prepare them for anything that might lie ahead. She noticed how often Mrs. Sydenstricker went to the window to look out at the river where, when the time came to escape, a red flag would be raised as a signal.

Chushi, the cook, came into the room one morning with tea for all of them set on a bamboo tray. As he poured the tea into each small cup, he spoke softly.

A look of fear spread across Pearl's face.

"What is he saying?" Mrs. Sydenstricker asked Pearl. No one in the family spoke Chinese as well as Pearl did, not even her mother. "Something about Shanxi?"

"They've killed almost fifty Christians there," Pearl said.

"Oh no!" her mother murmured.

The cook spoke again.

This time Pearl dropped to the floor and hugged him around the knees.

"What is it, darling?"

"He said he must leave us. He fears for our lives. And his own for associating with us," she cried.

"Of course," Mr. Sydenstricker said. "He should go."

After Chushi left, Pearl cried softly for some time in the hot, still room.

Mrs. Sydenstricker paced, walking from her chair to the window and back again, over and over, almost desperately.

Felix watched her go to look out the window once again. But this time her back stiffened, and she turned from the window with her face covered with relief.

"The flag is up!" she said. "It's time."

Just as they'd rehearsed, they all scrambled to their feet and ran to get their things. All except Mr. Sydenstricker, who refused to evacuate Zhenjiang.

With Mrs. Sydenstricker in the lead and Wang Amah carrying Grace, they walked out the back door, through the veranda, and down the emerald-green hills. As they passed the small, mud farmhouses that dotted the landscape, Felix begged Maisie to forgive him.

"Please," he said. "I did it so we could get home. I'll never do anything without talking to you first again, I promise. Just forgive me."

Maisie kept walking as if she didn't hear him. When Pearl had asked Maisie why she was ignoring Felix, Maisie had said, "Because he's a sneak, that's why!" But deep down, she knew it was more than the fact that he'd given Pearl that box without Maisie there. More and more it felt to Maisie like Felix didn't need her. Back in Newport, he had Jim Duncan and Lily Goldberg. It used to be the two of them and everyone else.

Now it felt like it was just her alone and everyone else. Why couldn't they have given Pearl the jade box together? Why did he have to do everything on his own?

The people working in the rice paddies barely looked up at the group of foreigners passing them. White geese walked beside them, their wings fluttering.

Finally, they reached the river where the boat waited for them. They boarded in silence, each of them staring back at the city they were leaving behind.

When the boat had traveled far enough for the city to disappear completely from view, Mrs. Sydenstricker let out a deep sigh.

"Shanghai," she said. She smiled. "Shanghai," she said again, louder.

◆ CHAPTER EIGHT ◆

Shanghai

"Shanghai doesn't feel like China at all," Pearl said sadly.

Pearl was right. Shanghai in 1900 was an open city, free to trade with other countries like Britain and France and the United States. As a result, it seemed more European than Chinese. For Maisie and Felix, Shanghai was fancy and exotic. They loved the large international ships docked on the Huangpu River and all of the sailors in their different country's uniforms. The streets of Shanghai were lined with shops selling imports from England and the United States: perfume, silk stockings, lingerie; cashmere scarves, leather boots and coats; wine in dusty wooden cases. Walking down the broad boulevard, they both liked to window-shop. If Maisie had forgiven him, Felix knew that they would have even more fun. But she continued to completely ignore him.

For Pearl, who had never even seen running water until they settled into a boardinghouse on Bubbling Well Road, all of the opulence of Shanghai made her homesick for Horse Street and the veranda that looked out over the Yangtze River.

"I hate it here," she would say repeatedly throughout the day.

Felix tried to hide his excitement at seeing yet another new place. He didn't want Pearl to feel even worse.

But Maisie kept trying to point out all of the positive things about Shanghai.

"I, for one, like being able to sit in a bathtub with cool water on these awful, hot days," Maisie said.

Pearl stared at her long and hard.

"You're used to that, though, aren't you? Coming from Shanghai in the first place," Pearl said.

Maisie had forgotten their story of running away from their parents in Shanghai and hopping on a junk to Zhenjiang.

"I am used to it," Maisie said. "Yes."

"But you don't seem to have any idea where anything in the city is," Pearl said, narrowing her blue eyes. "And neither does Felix."

Maisie chewed her bottom lip, trying to think up a good answer.

"You didn't come from Shanghai, did you?" Pearl asked.

When Maisie didn't answer, Pearl said, "It's all right. I won't tell."

🌱 🌱 🌱 🌱 🌱

More and more, Mrs. Sydenstricker talked about America and how safe they would be there. Sighing as she filled the bathtub for Pearl and Grace, she told them about how back home in West Virginia they would have running water and electric lights and all of the things they'd lived so long without.

"But what about Amah?" Pearl cried. "What about our little house and—"

"*Shhhh*," her mother said. "Your father isn't about to leave China."

Mr. Sydenstricker stayed in Zhenjiang all of that summer. He continued to wear a suit and his preacher's collar and to preach in the streets. Every time someone came to the boardinghouse on Bubbling Well Road with news, the family feared it would be news of his death. Despite being attacked with stones and sticks, he managed to avoid serious injuries.

One hot August evening, Mrs. Sydenstricker took Pearl, Maisie, and Felix to the Astor House Hotel in the Hongkou District. The Astor House Hotel was world famous, the most elegant hotel in Shanghai. In all of the Far East. Every important person in Shanghai met there at eleven in the morning to discuss world affairs and the problems in China. Tonight, a ball was being held at the Astor House Hotel, and Mrs. Sydenstricker wanted to see the women's gowns and furs as they arrived.

At first, Pearl refused to go.

"Please come, Pearl," Felix pleaded. "It won't be as much fun without you."

"Who knows what we'll see there," Maisie said. "Maybe something you can use in one of your stories."

"I only tell stories about China," Pearl said. But she softened a bit that Maisie thought of her as a storyteller.

"But this is part of China, too," Maisie added.

"A terrible part," Pearl said.

She put on her red hat with the gold Buddhas and tucked her thick, blond hair beneath it. Here in Shanghai, she didn't need to hide her blond hair. It was perfectly all right for her to wear it down. Maisie was happy to, but Pearl insisted on that hat.

🜊   🜊   🜊   🜊   🜊

They stood on the banks of the Huangpu River and stared across it to downtown Shanghai. Its hustle and bustle reminded Maisie of New York City.

"Look," Mrs. Sydenstricker said, stopping.

Her hand swept the air as if to take in everything that lay in front of them.

"This is the skyline of Shanghai," she said. She sounded as awestruck as Maisie and Felix felt.

Mrs. Sydenstricker first pointed out the wooden bridge that stretched across the Huangpu River.

"That's the Garden Bridge—" she began.

But Pearl interrupted her. "*Waibaidu Qiao*," she corrected.

Her mother laughed. Normally she would have scolded Pearl for being rude, but it was clear that Mrs. Sydenstricker was so happy to be here that she forgave Pearl immediately.

"My little jewel of the East," she said.

Then Mrs. Sydenstricker pointed out the large post office, the Richards Hotel, and the imposing and elegant Astor House Hotel, which was the largest of the three buildings.

As they stood there, the streetlights came on, and she sighed happily.

"Do you know that Shanghai is called the City without Nights? It's the first city here to have electric lights, and more than half of them are in the Astor House Hotel," she explained dreamily.

They crossed the street, past Chinese people in long robes with pigtails down their backs and Westerners in suits and dresses.

The Astor House Hotel was enormous, made up of four brick buildings connected by elaborate stone passageways. The front of the hotel was illuminated by large, red Chinese lanterns. Chinese men, dressed in red-and-white uniforms with gold fringe on their shoulders, stood stiffly at the doors. In metal urns along the entryway, fires burned in different colors: blue, orange, green, and violet. Although the hotel reminded Maisie and Felix of fancy hotels they had seen in New York and Newport, the Astor House Hotel emitted a different aura. It was old-fashioned and regal, an interesting combination of East and West.

A small crowd already waited at the entrance, and Mrs. Sydenstricker and the children joined them.

In no time, elegant horse-drawn carriages began to arrive. The horses were shiny and wore ornate silk on their heads. They walked in high steps, their hooves clacking against the stones like music. The carriages were polished to a bright sheen, with gold trim and lush-red or emerald-green or rich-yellow interiors. From them stepped beautiful women wearing fitted ball gowns and fur stoles. Chinese footmen appeared seemingly out of nowhere to help them out of the carriages. The women were followed by men in tuxedos and tall, silk top hats.

Maisie watched Mrs. Sydenstricker's face as she took it all in. She seemed filled with such longing that Maisie wished she could take her back to the United States immediately. If she knew how to get back. If she were speaking to her brother, she would whisper this to him. She would ask him what he thought happened to Pearl and her family. Maisie wanted to do this desperately, but she just couldn't let herself forgive him.

"Maisie?" Pearl was saying. "Mother's asking if we'd like to get tea at some dreadful British tea shop nearby."

"Oh. Sure," Maisie said.

She caught sight of Felix watching her hopefully as if he'd read her mind and knew how close she'd come to confiding her thoughts about the Sydenstrickers to him. As they followed Pearl's mother away from the Astor House Hotel, Maisie made a point of glaring at Felix just so he knew that she did not have any intention of forgiving him.

土　土　土　土　土

Pearl liked only one thing about Shanghai: the parks. Even in the heat and humidity of summer, the parks' grass stayed bright green and flowers managed to bloom. Felix liked the lotus flowers that seemed to float in the ponds in all of the parks, and Maisie pointed out all the different peonies that grew everywhere in different sizes and colors from white to pink to violet to one that looked almost black.

"You're a true Pickworth," Felix told her one day as they walked across a park with an unusual amount of peonies.

Their great-great-grandfather Phinneas Pickworth had cultivated the Pickworth peony, a hot-pink variety that filled the gardens at Elm Medona.

"What's a Pickworth?" Pearl asked.

Felix explained about Phinneas and Elm Medona.

"You mean you're rich?" Pearl said, surprised.

"I thought you were poor runaways."

"We are," Felix said. "We live up in the servants' quarters."

"It's dreadful," Maisie said. Of course, she thought just about anywhere was better than Newport and Elm Medona.

"I'm worried that we're going to leave," Pearl said. "Mother talks about it all the time."

"Leave Shanghai?" Maisie asked, concerned. "Or leave China?"

"China," Pearl said sadly.

What would she and Felix do if the Sydenstrickers left China? Unlike the other times they'd time traveled, Maisie had not thought much about how or when to get home. If Pearl and her family left, what would she and Felix do?

"Well," Felix said, "if you leave, I suppose we would go home, too."

"How did you get to Zhenjiang?" Pearl asked, delighted with a possible tale of adventure.

"It's complicated," Maisie said.

Pearl didn't ask any more questions. She was content to let her imagination fill in the blanks so she could make up her own stories.

Pausing to admire her favorite statue in this park, a tiny, stone boy holding an umbrella, she said, *"Nî hao xiaô haí ér."*

"What did you say?" Felix asked, relieved that Pearl wasn't pursuing her questioning.

"I said, 'Hello, little boy!'"

"Oh," Felix said. "How would I say 'Hello, friend'?"

Maisie rolled her eyes. "Or, 'Hello, Lily'?"

"*Pangyou nî hao,*" Pearl said. "That's 'Hello, friend.' But who is this Lily?"

"Nobody," Felix muttered, flushing with embarrassment.

By now they had reached the small zoo in the middle of the park. Pearl told Maisie and Felix to stay there and look at the animals while she went to arrange a surprise for the three of them. The zoo had kangaroos and monkeys and brightly colored parrots, a strange menagerie of animals that all looked pretty miserable. Felix thought about the Central Park Zoo, how his father sometimes took them there on Saturday mornings in time to watch the seals get fed. He used to worry about one of the polar bears that used to pace in a perfect square, tracing the four invisible sides. In his mind, Felix could still feel what it had been like to be little enough to sit on his father's shoulders, to ride high enough to see above the crowd at the zoo, to see the penguins in the distance. If he closed his eyes right now, he could perfectly picture the small bald spot on the top of his father's head, the pink scalp peeking through.

"Maisie," Felix said, his stomach clenching.

She pretended not to hear.

"Maisie," he said again, this time grabbing her shoulder and forcing her to face him.

"We need to go back," he said.

At first she looked confused as if he meant they needed to leave the zoo and go back to the boardinghouse on Bubbling Well Road. But then she understood that he meant *back*—to Newport and Elm Medona.

"No," she said, shaking his hand from her shoulder.

"Please," Felix said. "Just hear me out."

She narrowed her eyes at him defiantly but didn't walk away.

"As far as we know, when we get back it will still be the Christmas party, right?"

"I suppose so," she said slowly. "And your girlfriend will be standing in The Treasure Chest where you brought her without me."

He waved his hand as if to erase her words. "It will be December 9. Like two weeks before Dad is due to arrive."

"So?" Maisie said, crossing her arms over her chest.

"So if we go home now, we'll be like fifteen days away from seeing him again. The longer we stay here, the longer it will be before we get to see him. And Maisie," Felix added, his voice cracking, "I want to see Dad. I want to start counting down those fifteen days."

She didn't say anything, but Felix could tell she was considering what he'd told her. Here in China in 1900, days still took twenty-four hours to pass. Each day spent here felt like another day away from getting to see their father, even if back home time was standing still.

In the distance, they could see Pearl approaching. They could see her red hat with the gold Buddhas and a big smile on her face.

"How do we do it?" Maisie said softly.

It was true. They had figured out some things: that they needed to both hold the object in The Treasure Chest, that they needed to give the object to the right person. But they had not yet figured out how to get back home. The first time, they had tried to both hold the object again as if it might work in reverse. Nothing. The second time they had returned so suddenly that they had no idea what had brought them back.

"We need to re-create exactly what was happening both times when we traveled back," Felix said.

Pearl was waving something at them.

"I have enough yuan to ride the tortoise!" she shouted.

"Did she say tortoise?" Maisie repeated. "Like a giant turtle?"

Once again, Felix grabbed his sister's shoulder and turned her so that she faced him.

"Think!" he said, hearing the desperation in his voice.

But there was no time to think. Pearl had arrived and was tugging at their hands, pulling them across the park where a giant tortoise sat in the hot Shanghai sun, dry and brown and wrinkly, giving rides to children for a couple of yuan. Maisie and Felix had no choice but to stand in the line with Pearl and wait their turn. Then, first Felix, then Maisie, and finally Pearl, stepped through the small gate into the dirt circle where the tortoise waited.

An olive-skinned man with a big mustache took the yuan, then motioned for them to sit on the tortoise. Its shell was as hard and brown as a horse's saddle, its neck long and thick. The tortoise swung its head back, its small, beady eyes staring blankly. The man hit the tortoise with a switch of a green branch, and it began to move slowly around the circle.

Felix didn't tell Pearl that he didn't especially enjoy sitting on that tortoise. It smelled faintly like sewage, and it was inhumane to ride a tortoise. His father had explained to him a long time ago one of those Saturday afternoons at the zoo that zoos used to be cruel to animals, caging them and even shackling them in place. What good would it do to tell Pearl that this poor tortoise belonged in a nice pond somewhere? She had been so excited to pay for their rides, he didn't want to make her feel bad. For a moment, he found himself holding his breath, hoping that Maisie didn't offend Pearl. But his sister stayed quiet and thoughtful during their tortoise ride and the whole way back to Bubbling Well Road.

· CHAPTER NINE ·

How to Get Home

Felix woke to a rough shaking. He opened his eyes and found Maisie kneeling beside him and trying hard to wake him up.

"I haven't slept at all," she whispered.

"How come?" he asked through a yawn.

"Because I've been trying to figure out how we got back the other times," she said.

"And?" Felix asked. He reached for his glasses. Somehow wearing them helped make him more alert.

"And we did nothing. Nothing at all," Maisie said, her voice rising.

"*Shhh*," Felix said.

He glanced around the small room to be sure

Pearl was still asleep. When he saw that she was, he got out of bed and tiptoed toward the door. Maisie followed him, and together they went down the wooden stairs, through the front parlor with its worn furniture, and out into the hot Shanghai night.

The air was sweet with the smell of flowers that neither of them could name. The black sky seemed to drip stars. Maisie and Felix stood in their cotton pants and tunics—his navy blue and hers powder blue—gazing up. Shanghai was a noisy city, always bursting with ships' horns, carriage wheels, vendors hawking their goods, and all of the other sounds of city life. But out here, this late at night, all they could hear was the constant chirp of crickets. Standing there, they both felt the vastness of China stretching out before them. Felix almost told Maisie that he felt small, like a drop of water in history, both insignificant and somehow important.

But Maisie was already getting agitated.

"I've gone over it a million times," she said. "At Clara's, we were outside talking and then without any warning we were back home. And we were in the cemetery with Alexander and—same thing. All of a sudden we're back."

"We're missing something," Felix said.

He had thought about it, too, and he remembered it exactly as Maisie did.

"*They* had the objects," Maisie said.

"Definitely."

"I remember Clara telling us about her aunt, the nurse, right before."

Felix nodded. "That's right."

"And we were standing in the cemetery with Alexander and he was talking about having been orphaned so young and working for Beekman and Cruger."

"Okay," Felix said, wishing he had a pen to make notes. "They had the objects. We both were with them." He thought hard. "Time of day maybe?"

"No," Maisie said, disappointed. "Clara was in the afternoon, and Alexander was superearly in the morning. Remember, I followed him out there at dawn when he used to go and study?" The memory made her feel sad. Maisie missed listening to Alexander, and she knew that Felix missed Clara, too.

Felix sighed. "So Clara was talking about her aunt, and Alexander was talking about his parents . . ."

They looked at each other hopelessly.

"Maybe it's out of our control?" Felix offered.

"Maybe we go back when we're done."

"Done with what?" Maisie said, frustrated.

"I don't know. Maybe we help them somehow? In some other way?"

Now Maisie sighed. "That's not it. If anything, they help us. They take us in and feed us. They give us clothes."

"And tortoise rides," Felix said, smiling.

But Maisie didn't smile back at him. "Joke all you want, but we'll never get home if we don't figure this out." Her face changed, and then she added softly, "I want to count down the twelve days, too."

As soon as she said the words out loud, Maisie got hit with the strongest feeling of missing her father that she had ever felt. All these months since the divorce, she had thought about him and missed him like crazy. She'd spent so much time homesick for their old life in New York that she hadn't even made one friend in Newport. But ever since Felix had explained why he thought they should go back, Maisie had started to realize that her father was becoming a fuzzy memory. Sometimes she couldn't remember what his voice sounded like. Sometimes it took her several minutes before his face changed from blurry to sharp in her mind. Every time these things happened, she panicked. Her heart beat too fast, and she couldn't catch her breath until she could bring him back to her.

Seeing the look on his sister's face, Felix said, "Don't worry. We'll figure it out."

She looked at him doubtfully.

"We figured out how to time travel in the first place, right?" he reminded her. "I'm sure we can figure out how to get back."

土　土　土　土　土

Sometimes it felt like all there was to do in Shanghai was take cold baths to cool off, go to the parks and public gardens, and window-shop. As the days passed, even Wang Amah's relenting to unbandage her feet and show them to Pearl, Maisie, and Felix had lost some of its thrill. It was hot. Blistering, relentlessly hot. And the heat made everyone cranky. Pearl began most of her sentences with "In *real* China . . ." To Pearl, Shanghai was not China at all.

One day, as they walked through one of the parks, Pearl stopped suddenly.

"What's wrong?" Felix asked her.

Angrily, she marched over to a sign posted on the grass.

"No dogs or Chinamen," Pearl read. "No dogs or Chinamen," she repeated loudly. "Like the

Chinese people are no better than dogs? Like the British aren't here because the Chinese said they could be here?"

Her voice grew louder and louder, and her face grew red.

"I hate it here!" Pearl shouted. "I hate Shanghai, and I want to go home!"

Before Felix could put his arm around her shoulders and calm her down, Maisie cried, "Me too! I want to go home."

In an instant, the two girls fell into each other's arms, sobbing.

"Oh no," Felix said helplessly.

For some reason, that made them cry even harder.

He glanced around as if he might find help somewhere. But the businessmen walking briskly through the park didn't even seem to notice them. A round nanny in a white uniform pushing a fancy carriage frowned at them but didn't pause.

Then something in the distance caught Pearl's eye.

"Look!" she said, sniffling and pulling away from Maisie.

"What?" Maisie asked.

Pearl pointed to a statue at the end of the path.

"It's Kwan Yin," she explained. "She's the Goddess of Mercy."

Maisie did not look impressed.

"She hears the cries of the world," Pearl said hopefully. "Surely she'll hear ours and help us all get back home."

Pearl took off running toward the statue.

"Well," Felix said, "it wouldn't hurt."

Reluctantly, Maisie walked with Felix down the path.

When Pearl saw them, she grinned.

"I should have been asking her all along," she said.

From her pocket, she pulled out the small jade box that Felix had given her.

"I carry it everywhere," she added. "Remember, Felix? You said that no matter where I went, I could take this little box filled with the earth from home with me?"

"May I see that?" Maisie asked Pearl.

Pearl handed the box to her, and Maisie held it tightly in her hand, closing her eyes and concentrating hard.

When she opened her eyes again, she looked around, clearly disappointed.

"I thought . . . ," she began.

"Did you think you could pray to her and open

your eyes and be home?" Pearl teased.

But Maisie looked at Felix and said, "Yes. Well, I hoped."

"It doesn't work that fast!" Pearl laughed. "You're getting as bad as Amah. Next thing I know, you'll believe a magic rabbit lives on the moon."

Maisie's eyes took in the statue in front of her: the flowing, green robe, the willow twig in one hand, and the vase dripping dew in the other. Even though she didn't believe in all this Chinese superstition, maybe praying to Kwan Yin would help. It wouldn't hurt, she decided.

She took a deep breath and thought as hard as she could, "Kwan Yin, do you hear me crying to go home?"

The stone face stared back at her.

⟟　⟟　⟟　⟟　⟟

When they got back to the boardinghouse on Bubbling Well Road, Mrs. Sydenstricker was waiting anxiously outside for them. As soon as she saw them turn the corner, she smiled and ran to meet them.

"Pearl! Wonderful news from your father!"

Pearl's eyes glistened with joy. "We're going home!" she said. "Finally!"

Felix saw Mrs. Sydenstricker's face fall. She

reminded him of his own mother when she was about to disappoint him.

"Pearl," Mrs. Sydenstricker said, putting her hand on Pearl's arm. "I'm sorry. It's time for us to go to our real home."

"Real home?" Pearl said.

"He's booked us passage on a steamship to San Francisco," Mrs. Sydenstricker said.

"San Francisco?" Pearl said, her eyes darkening.

"Yes!" her mother said. "And from there on to West Virginia."

"America isn't home," Pearl said angrily.

"It is," her mother said. "It will be, Pearl. I promise."

Maisie felt like she was listening to her own mother right before the Christmas party when she'd been complaining about not having any friends in Newport. *You will soon, sweetie,* she'd said. *I promise.* Her words hadn't made Maisie feel better. Not really. How could a mother promise something that seemed impossible to get?

Still, Maisie said to Pearl, "I never thought I would feel at home anywhere except New York City. When we moved to Newport, I was totally miserable. I hated it. New York was my home, not that awful place."

"And now you're happy there?" Pearl said, knowing the answer.

Maisie hesitated.

But Felix jumped right in. "I love Newport now, Pearl," he said. "At first, I was unhappy there. But before I knew it, I had friends and I fell in love with the harbor and all the sailboats there."

Mrs. Sydenstricker smiled at him gratefully.

"It's taken me longer," Maisie said. "But slowly I'm getting used to it. Maybe I'll always miss our old apartment and the streets around that neighborhood. Maybe I'll always want the sounds of the city outside all around me. But that doesn't mean I'm not warming up to Newport."

"See, Pearl?" her mother said. "They know exactly how you feel."

At that, Pearl's eyes flared with anger.

"I want to go to Zhenjiang. That's my home!"

She didn't wait for her mother or Maisie or Felix to answer. Instead, Pearl ran off, away from the boardinghouse.

Maisie turned to Felix.

"I think our wishes got mixed up," she said. "Now what are we going to do?"

土 土 土 土 土

That night in bed, Felix heard Pearl crying softly.

"Don't cry," he told her. "Maybe you'll come back when it's safe."

"Mother hates it here," Pearl said sadly. "She won't come back unless Father makes her."

"Why does she hate it so much?" Maisie asked.

Pearl sighed. "Because of my sisters and brothers."

"The ones who . . ." Felix hesitated.

"Yes," Pearl said. "The ones in heaven."

"Did you know them, Pearl?" Maisie asked. "Or did they . . . was it . . . before you were born?"

They were all sitting up now, their thin, cotton blankets around their shoulders. The moon lit the little room and shone full and white in the window.

"First Maude went to heaven. Then Arthur. He got malaria while Father was up north, and they took him by boat to bury beside Maudie. But Mother got cholera, too, and the doctor thought she would die. Father took over the care of Edith— Mother was too sick. And poor Edith contracted cholera and died, just two weeks after Arthur."

Both Felix and Maisie were speechless at this story of loss, their eyes filled with tears.

"Mother blamed the heat of summer. The mosquitoes. The flies. The dirty water. After Maudie died, she used to beg Father to spend

summers near the sea. Or to return back to
America for good. But he refused. When Arthur
and Edith died that summer—this was before I
was born—Mother threatened to leave Father. She
couldn't bear to lose anything more."

"But here you are, still," Felix said. "He
wouldn't leave."

"They went back to America. And I was born
while they were there. But Father only agreed to
go there because the doctor told him that Mother
was losing her mind from grief. You know, it is
possible to die from a broken heart," Pearl said.

"Your poor, poor mother," Maisie said.

"Our sorrow wasn't over, though," Pearl
continued. Her voice had an edge of pain to it
as she spoke now. "My little brother, Clyde, died
several months before you arrived. He got this
awful cough, and his coloring was like ashes. I had
it, too, and was in my bed burning with fever when
I heard a woman screaming. At first I thought
it was coming from our neighbor's. But then I
recognized the voice. It was Wang Amah. That's
when I knew."

At the same time, Maisie and Felix reached for
Pearl's hand, each of them holding one of hers in
their own.

"Father was away up north when Clyde went to

heaven. But he came home for the funeral," Pearl added.

They were silent for a moment, then Pearl said, "He was my little buddy. We used to play on the hillside outside our house and go to Horse Street with Wang Amah and tell each other the most marvelous stories. Mother insisted that we leave the city in the summer, so we would go to the mountains, to Kuling, where we had a small cabin. I do wish there hadn't been so much trouble this summer, or you would have both come with us. The trip up Mount Lu is thrilling. Four pairs of men carry us by bamboo poles on chairs all the way up the mountain. Along the way we stop in the little villages for tea, and the men hang awnings across the poles to keep the sun off us. Do you know, even in the summer it's cool up there? And the water in the stream is so clean we can drink straight from it. Mother felt relaxed when we were there. Safe," she said, her voice heavy with sadness.

"But this is so terrible!" Maisie blurted.

Pearl nodded. "Clyde was so brave," she said. "He knew he was dying, and he told us that he was leaving our house to go to his home in heaven."

At this, both Maisie and Felix could not hold back their tears.

Pearl tried to soothe them, murmuring, "There, there," and reminding them that her mother had Grace now, and also that there was an older brother Edgar, who was safe and in school in America.

But they had never heard such a sad story or met anyone who had had to bear so much loss. Maisie's own sadness over moving away and their parents' divorce seemed selfish in comparison.

"I do think they are all together in heaven," Pearl said. "But meanwhile we have to appreciate what we have here on earth, don't we? And aren't you two the luckiest people in the world? Twins! You've been together since before you were even born!"

That made them smile.

"Our mother says in our sonogram, we were holding hands," Maisie said.

"Your what?" Pearl asked.

"Oops," Maisie said. Of course, she realized, sonograms weren't invented yet in 1900.

Pearl leaned closer to Maisie and Felix.

"I didn't know Maude or Artie or Edith," she told them. "But I knew my little brother, Clyde, and I loved him more than anything. You two have each other, and you have to always remember how special that is. You have to treasure it, always."

Maisie let out a big sob and threw her arms around Felix's neck.

"I'm so sorry," she cried. "I've been so mean to you."

Felix was hugging her back just as hard.

"No, no," he was saying. "I was thoughtless. I'll never go behind your back again."

They grew so emotional and cried so hard to each other and repeated "I'm sorry" and "I love you" so many times, that neither of them realized that the air grew heavy with the smells of Christmas trees and cinnamon and bread baking or that they were being lifted up, up, up.

When they finally parted, they heard Lily Goldberg say in a confused voice, "What in the world are you two doing?"

Maisie and Felix blinked. Then they blinked again.

"Oh," Maisie said happily. "We're home."

· CHAPTER TEN ·

A Cold Wind

Lily Goldberg stared down at Maisie and Felix, who lay splayed out on the floor of The Treasure Chest.

"Well, of course you're home," Lily said, shaking her head, annoyed. "Where else would you be?"

They looked at each other and grinned.

"Can we go get dinner now?" Lily asked. She was wearing that dissatisfied face that Felix liked so much.

"Sure," he said, helping Maisie to her feet. "Are you hungry?" he asked his sister.

Maisie nodded. "Don't they have roast beef and stuff?"

Lily wrinkled her nose in disgust. "Ew," she said. "I'm a vegetarian."

"They'll have something for you, too," Felix assured her.

"Where . . . ," Lily said under her breath, looking around. "Where in the world . . . ?"

"What?" Felix said.

"That little jade box," Lily said. "Where is it?"

"Oh," Maisie said. "Don't worry about it."

"Are you sure?" Lily said, unconvinced.

"We're sure," Felix said.

They began to walk toward the door, Lily still keeping an eye out for the box, when the doorway filled with the Blond Woman.

"Caught you!" she said, pointing a quivering finger at them. Her overplucked, overarched eyebrows shot upward, and her thin lips set into a tight line.

"Uh-oh," Maisie said.

"*Uh-oh* is right," the Blond Woman said.

Up close like this she looked even scarier with those eyebrows and lips and her beady, blue eyes flaring angrily.

"We just—" Felix began.

Lily stepped forward, her hand extended.

"Lily Goldberg," she said. "I take full

responsibility for being here. I've never been in one of these mansions before, and I wandered up here by myself. They just came looking for me."

The Blond Woman narrowed her already small eyes.

"In fact," Lily said, her hand still waiting for the Blond Woman to shake it, "they were just explaining how this room is—"

"Off-limits," Maisie interjected.

Felix was nodding his head like a bobblehead. "Off-limits," he repeated.

"Well," the Blond Woman said, thinking.

Lily lifted her hand slightly as if to remind her she was supposed to shake it.

Reluctantly, the Blond Woman did.

"Now that we've got her," Maisie said, "we're going to go downstairs and get some food."

Lily smiled up at the Blond Woman. "Roast beef," she said with false enthusiasm.

"Well," the Blond Woman said again.

They didn't wait for her to think about it any longer. Instead, the three of them hurried past her, walking fast down the hall to the Grand Staircase and the party going on below.

"That was great!" Maisie said as they moved down the marble stairs.

"Yeah," Felix said. "You were amazing."

At the bottom of the stairs, he touched Lily's arm lightly.

"*Xiè xie,*" he said.

"Huh?" Lily said.

"That's Chinese," Felix explained. "For thank you."

"It is?" Lily said. "You know some Chinese?"

"A little," Felix said.

She looked at him, impressed.

"Oh, yeah," Maisie said. "He can even write Chinese characters in beautiful calligraphy."

"Wow," Lily said.

Felix was beaming. "Confucius says, 'He who does not revere letters is no better than a blind buffalo.'"

Lily's eyes shone. "What else does Confucius say, Felix?"

"Let's get some food and I'll tell you," he said.

土 土 土 土 土

The day after the party, their mother took Maisie and Felix to visit Great-Aunt Maisie. The Island Retirement Center was decorated for Christmas with a big, artificial tree in the lobby. Big, blue ornaments hung from it and gold garland wrapped around its branches. Gold garland and cardboard Santas appeared just about everywhere, on desks and doorways and windows.

"It's certainly festive," their mother said
unconvincingly.

They all felt a little guilty living in Elm
Medona, with its lavish Christmas decorations and
the VIP party, while poor Great-Aunt Maisie was
confined here.

As they walked down the hall to her room,
their mother said, "Now remember, she's been
failing a bit these last few weeks. Don't rile her
up."

"Oh," Felix said, "I have a feeling she'll be
doing great."

His mother tousled his hair. "My optimist,"
she said.

The door to Great-Aunt Maisie's room was
open, with one of those cardboard Santas tacked
on it.

When they walked in, the room was empty. The
bed was neatly made, with Great-Aunt Maisie's
favorite ivory cashmere throw blanket folded
at the foot of the bed. A large, white amaryllis
bloomed in a bamboo planter on her night table,
and another one sat on the small, round table by
the window beside the silver bell she used to call
the staff. The curtains were open to let in the
morning sun, and the room smelled of Great-
Aunt Maisie's perfume.

Despite the cozy feeling of the room, Maisie and Felix's mother looked upset.

"Oh dear," she said, worried. "I hope nothing has happened to her."

She picked up the silver bell and rang it lightly. When Great-Aunt Maisie used it, she gave it a firm shake that pierced their ears.

A nurse in a mauve uniform came in.

"I knew that wasn't your aunt calling," she said. "She practically breaks my eardrums with that thing."

"I'm sorry," their mother said. "I just . . . I mean . . . where is she?"

The nurse shook her head in wonder. "It's the darnedest thing," she said. "For weeks now she's been slipping again. Not as bad as she was when she first came in here. But you know, getting more and more frail. Then last night, she comes walking down the hall without her walker! I jumped up, thinking maybe she was sleepwalking or worse, but she says, 'I'm just stretching my legs,' and when I tried to help her, she actually pushed me away. It was so great to see her being so feisty!"

Although their mother looked surprised, Felix knew for certain what he had suspected was true: Every time they time traveled, it made Great-Aunt Maisie stronger.

"And where is she now?" their mother was asking.

"She insisted on going out to the garden," the nurse said. "By herself."

"But she'll catch pneumonia out there," their mother said. "It's cold outside."

The nurse shrugged. "You try telling Maisie Pickworth what to do," she said.

"We'll go get her, Mom," Felix offered. "You can make her some tea for when she comes inside. She'll like that."

"Good idea," their mother said, already reaching for the kettle. "She does like her Earl Grey."

土 土 土 土 土

Maisie and Felix found Great-Aunt Maisie sitting on one of the stone benches in the garden behind the Island Retirement Center. The garden looked out over Narragansett Bay, but Great-Aunt Maisie had her eyes closed and her face tilted up toward the sun. She wore her usual face powder and rouged cheeks and red lipstick, and she had on a big, reddish fur coat with long, black gloves that had tiny pearl buttons up their sides.

Maisie and Felix stood uncertainly in front of her, not wanting to disturb her.

"I know you're here," Great-Aunt Maisie said without opening her eyes. "I'm not that dotty."

"You just looked so . . ." Felix searched for the word.

"Content," Maisie finished for him.

Great-Aunt Maisie opened her eyes then.

"That's because I am content," she said in a strong voice. She had a rich person's accent, slightly British sounding and very confident.

Her eyes twinkled. "You two had an adventure, I think?"

"Oh, Great-Aunt Maisie," Maisie said. "We went to China!"

Great-Aunt Maisie clapped her hands together gleefully. "China! How marvelous." She pointed one of her slender fingers at them. "Confucius?"

They looked at her, confused.

"Mao Tse-tung?"

When they didn't answer, she said sharply, "Who did you meet there?"

"Oh!" Felix said. "Pearl Sydenstricker."

"Pearl Sydenstricker," Great-Aunt Maisie said with a laugh. "Do you know who she is?"

Felix shook his head.

"Pearl Sydenstricker grew up to be Pearl Buck," Great-Aunt Maisie said as if the name Pearl Buck meant anything to them.

When she saw that it didn't, she shook her head in disgust.

"What do they teach children in school these days?" she said. "Haven't you read *The Good Earth*?"

"No," Maisie said.

"But you've heard of it, of course," Great-Aunt Maisie said.

"No," Felix admitted.

"You poor, ignorant things," Great-Aunt Maisie said. "*The Good Earth* is a novel by Pearl S. Buck that was published in 1931 and won the Pulitzer Prize for the Novel in 1932."

"Pearl won the Pulitzer Prize?" Felix said.

"*And* the Nobel Prize for Literature in 1938," Great-Aunt Maisie said. "The first American woman to do that," she added.

"She does love to tell stories," Maisie said.

"What's it about?" Felix asked.

"I shouldn't tell you, should I?" Great-Aunt Maisie said. "You should both read it, I daresay."

"Please tell us," Felix asked.

"It's about life in a village in China before the revolution," Great-Aunt Maisie said. "And that's all I'll say. You need to read it to really understand it."

"I read a lot," Felix said softly.

"What do you read? Comic books?" She didn't wait for him to answer. "Well, now you'll have to

read your friend Pearl Buck's books, won't you?"
she said with a slight smile on her face.

"Yes," Felix said.

Even though he felt scolded, he didn't care.
Pearl had become a famous writer! A prizewinning
novelist! This made him so happy, he could ignore
Great-Aunt Maisie's comments.

"Great-Aunt Maisie?" Maisie was asking.

"What is it?" Great-Aunt Maisie said, pulling
the collar of her coat tighter around her against
the wind that was picking up.

"We can't figure out how to get home when
we're . . . away," Maisie said.

The wind whistled around them.

"You need to use your brain," Great-Aunt
Maisie said. "How do you *think* you get home?"

"We don't know," Maisie said, clearly disturbed
by Great-Aunt Maisie's curtness today.

"At first we thought we just needed to give the
object to the right person," Felix explained. "Like
we gave Pearl a jade box filled with dirt."

"And?" Great-Aunt Maisie said.

"That isn't how it works," Maisie said. "We
figured that out."

"This time, we were sitting up in bed, talking
with Pearl and all of a sudden we were on the floor
of The Treasure Chest," Felix said.

"Mmmm," Great-Aunt Maisie said. "Sitting up in bed. Talking."

"Right," Maisie said.

Great-Aunt Maisie looked at them as if she were waiting for something.

"Sitting?" Maisie guessed.

But Felix was already shaking his head.

"No," he said. "We were standing with Alexander in the cemetery."

"Well, talking then?" Maisie asked impatiently.

Great-Aunt Maisie didn't answer. She just sat there, waiting. The wind grew louder still, and now gray clouds raced across the sky, blocking the bright sun.

"Just tell us!" Maisie said.

"Why should I tell you what's as clear as the nose on your face?" Great-Aunt Maisie said.

"Wait," Felix said thoughtfully. "Pearl was telling us about her sisters and brothers who died. And Alexander was telling us about being an orphan."

"So?" Maisie said. "And Clara was telling us about her own aunt, the nurse."

A small smile crept across Great-Aunt Maisie's face.

"And?" she said.

Felix smiled, too. "They need to give us something as well, don't they?" he said. "We give them an object from The Treasure Chest, and they give us advice or a lesson of some kind. Something we need back home."

Maisie did not understand. "They didn't *give* us anything at all," she said.

But the more Felix thought about it, the clearer it became.

"But they did, Maisie," he said. "You were furious with me in China, and Pearl told us how important and precious siblings are. No sooner did she say that and we made up, then we were home."

"And Alexander told us how lucky we were to have our parents, even if they weren't together," Maisie remembered.

Felix nodded. "It was Clara who told us we should listen to you, Great-Aunt Maisie," he said.

"Ha!" Great-Aunt Maisie said. "I'm glad someone has some sense."

The trees began to practically bow in the increasing wind.

Great-Aunt Maisie shivered in her fur coat.

"I don't like this wind," she said, looking out toward the bay.

The water had turned from blue-green to

gray, and whitecaps now danced across it.

"Maybe we should go inside," Felix suggested.

"Something's coming," Great-Aunt Maisie said. "Something bad."

"No, no," Maisie said. "I think it's just a winter storm."

Great-Aunt Maisie stood. Her posture was perfect: her head held high, her back as straight as a ruler.

"We shall see," she said. "We shall see."

•CHAPTER ELEVEN•

A Surprise Visitor

"Mom?" Felix asked their mother in the car on the way back from visiting Great-Aunt Maisie. "How old is Great-Aunt Maisie, anyway?"

"Hmmm," their mother said. "Funny, but I don't really know."

"Do you think she's a hundred?" Maisie asked.

"No," their mother said. But then she said, "Well, maybe."

Their mother grew thoughtful.

"She has so much spunk, doesn't she?" she said with a small smile. "Hey! I just had a great idea."

"Uh-oh," Maisie said.

"She's feeling so well," their mother continued, "we should have her come home for Christmas."

The very idea made Felix uneasy. If Great-Aunt Maisie got anywhere near The Treasure Chest, who knew what she would do? Of course, she didn't have a shard from the Ming vase, and they had learned that they needed that to time travel. But what if she got a hold of theirs? Was it possible to go back in time alone? Felix thought he needed Maisie in order to do it, but who knew what Great-Aunt Maisie was capable of?

"I don't think that's a good idea," he said, elbowing his sister.

"Me neither. Where would she sleep?" Maisie asked. "How would she get up all those stairs? What if she got sick or something?"

"I'm going to call her doctor as soon as we get home and see if he'll approve it," their mother said as if they hadn't protested. "You know, when I was a very little girl, I had one Christmas at Elm Medona. I'll never forget eating at that enormous table in the dining room on the Pickworth china, those two *P*s looping together. It took four butlers to even move the chair so that I could climb onto it."

Their mother's eyes had grown dreamy as she talked.

"I'll never forget that Christmas. We had goose for dinner. And oysters and cheese soufflé."

"Great-Aunt Maisie won't want to come to Elm Medona," Maisie said. "It will make her sad."

"I know!" their mother said, still ignoring anything they offered. "I'll re-create that dinner for her."

"Goose?" Felix said miserably. "You're going to cook a goose?"

"And mincemeat pies and, oh! That's right, a plum pudding. The cook baked a ring into it, and whoever got the slice with that ring was going to have good luck."

Felix thought about flying the kite with Mr. Kung and Pearl, how it had lifted and dipped before it floated upward.

Their mother smiled at them in the rearview mirror.

"This is going to be a good Christmas after all," she said.

⼟　⼟　⼟　⼟　⼟

Over the next week, while Maisie and Felix fretted over how to keep Great-Aunt Maisie out of Elm Medona and The Treasure Chest, their mother studied cookbooks and made elaborate lists and menu ideas. Whenever they wandered past her, she looked up, happily dazed, and said things like, "I think that goose I had here as a child was stuffed with apples and prunes and chestnuts," or

"Did you know that the secret to a good soufflé is to resist the temptation to open the oven door while it's baking?"

On the last day of school before Christmas vacation, Maisie and Felix came home from school to find their mother sitting at the kitchen table with the Blond Woman.

"We haven't done anything wrong!" Maisie blurted as soon as she saw her.

The Blond Woman glared.

"Maisie, Felix," their mother said. "I invited Barbara here to discuss the possibility of actually having Christmas dinner in Elm Medona's dining room."

"It seems that if your great-aunt is in attendance, this can be arranged," the Blond Woman said, clearly unhappy about the rule.

Her double chin rested on the top of her light-blue turtleneck, quivering ever so slightly when she spoke. A navy-blue cardigan was tied jauntily around her shoulders. Maisie wondered if she had a closet full of sweaters, the sleeves already looped together, waiting for her.

"Barbara was just explaining all the rules to me," their mother said with false cheerfulness.

"Great," Felix said with his own false cheerfulness.

Their mother sighed. "This will make Great-Aunt Maisie so happy," she said.

"Well, we must keep Miss Pickworth happy," the Blond Woman said.

She rose, smoothing her khaki skirt as she did.

"So," their mother said, leading her to the door, "on Christmas Eve, we'll have hors d'oeuvres and wine at six, serve dinner at seven sharp, dessert by eight thirty, and finish up by nine or nine thirty."

"At the latest," the Blond Woman said firmly.

"At the very latest," their mother said agreeably.

From the window, Maisie and Felix watched as the Blond woman got into her fancy, foreign car and drove off. As soon as the sound of the engine disappeared into the distance, their mother let out a huge sigh.

"What an awful woman," she said. "Smug and bossy and obnoxious. But," she added, a smile spreading on her lips, "like all women like that, if you let her feel superior, she gives you exactly what you want."

"Mom," Felix said tentatively, "I know you have your heart set on this, but—"

She didn't hear him, though. She was

humming some song Maisie and Felix didn't
recognize and making notes in the notebook
she'd dedicated to Christmas Eve dinner.

⟊   ⟊   ⟊   ⟊   ⟊

On Christmas Eve morning, Maisie woke up
to the sound of something so familiar, and so
wonderful, that instead of groaning at the sun
or burrowing deeper under her covers, she lay
in bed with her eyes open and listened closely to
whatever was making her feel so good this early.

From the kitchen down the hall came the
smell of strong coffee and the murmur of voices.

Maisie's bedroom door opened, and Felix
practically bounded into her room. His cowlick
stuck up sharply and his glasses were perched on
the tip of his nose, both indications that he, too,
had been awakened.

"He's here," Felix said.

Maisie nodded.

But Felix was taking her hands now and
tugging her up and out of bed.

"I almost feel," she said, running her fingers
through her tangle of hair, "that if we walk in that
kitchen he'll disappear."

Felix understood. He, too, was overcome
by the feeling that these moments before they
went down the hall to the kitchen were precious

and practically magical.

But he assured his sister, "He won't disappear."

Together they walked slowly down the hall, the voices growing louder as they neared the kitchen.

At the sound of their footsteps, the voices stopped. Maisie and Felix stepped over the threshold into the kitchen, right into the waiting arms of their father. He scooped them both up at once and hugged them to him so tightly that for an instant they couldn't catch their breaths. Or was it being in his arms at last that caused that?

"You have both grown a mile," he murmured into the tops of their heads.

Maisie took a deep breath, inhaling their father's smells of Old Spice and turpentine and that unnamable scent that was just his alone.

Gently, he put them both down.

With his feet back on the floor, Felix gazed up the length of their father, all six feet four inches of him. Starting with those familiar hiking boots he wore every winter, scuffed and laced with bright-red laces, past his favorite worn jeans that seemed about to tear in places but managed to hold out year after year, to the slight swell of his stomach pushing against his denim shirt, to his five o'clock shadow sprinkled across his chin and cheeks, and then taking in his green eyes and tumble of dark curls just flecked with silver. Maybe there was a little more silver than the last time he'd seen him, Felix decided. But otherwise he was 100 percent their father, Jake Robbins.

He reached his long arm across to the counter and held up a Dunkin' Donuts bag.

"Plain with chocolate sprinkles for you," he said, handing a doughnut to Felix. "And a chocolate-glazed chocolate for you," he told Maisie.

Felix bit into his doughnut and wondered if anything had ever tasted sweeter.

"Jake," their mother said, and her voice startled both Maisie and Felix because they had forgotten all about her. "Napkins."

"Ah, yes," he said, winking at them. "The crumb patrol."

A bit of awkwardness settled between their mother and father as he rooted around for napkins and distributed them. That was when Maisie and Felix remembered that their parents were no longer married or in love. In fact, they didn't even like each other very much anymore.

"So," their father said, "I couldn't wait to see you guys, but I have to go check into the hotel and maybe catch a little shut-eye. I understand there's quite a shindig here tonight."

"But you can't go already!" Maisie said, spilling chocolate doughnut from her mouth.

"You just arrived," Felix said.

Their father turned toward their mother, who was standing in her old, green bathrobe, her arms folded tightly across her chest and her favorite doughnut—a plain cruller—left untouched on a napkin beside her.

"I could take them with me," he said carefully. "They could show me around town a bit."

"Please, Mom," Maisie pleaded.

"Well," their mother said, and they could see her trying to decide what to do. "I suppose I can handle all the dinner preparations."

"We'll even pick up Great-Aunt Maisie," their father said. "Deliver her here safe and sound."

"No later than six," their mother said sternly. "We have to start at six sharp or—"

"Six sharp," their father said gently.

"Well then," their mother said to Maisie and Felix. "What are you waiting for? Go and get dressed."

🜨 🜨 🜨 🜨 🜨

A day with their father, just the three of them, was better than any Christmas present Maisie or Felix could imagine. They bounced on the bed in his room at the Viking Hotel, and Maisie used all the free body lotion in the bathroom while Felix channel surfed on the flat-screen TV. Then they got in his rental car and led him past their school and Bannister's Wharf and First Beach, trying in a few hours to fill in all the weeks and months they'd lived without him. They had lunch at The Fisherman's Catch, big bowls of creamy clam chowder and stuffed quahogs, the two of them chattering the entire time and basking in having their father so near.

Walking back to the car, they ran into Jim Duncan and his grandparents, who were visiting from Saint Petersburg, Florida.

"This is my dad," Felix said, practically bursting with joy.

Their father and Jim shook hands, and then he shook hands with Jim's grandfather and grandmother, and they stood talking briefly about the weather in Florida compared to the weather here in Newport.

As if on cue, big, fat snowflakes began to drift lazily down, landing in their hair and eyelashes and coats.

Could today be any more perfect? Maisie thought, slipping her red, mittened hand into her father's big, woolly gloved one.

🪨 🪨 🪨 🪨 🪨

"I thought you were out of the picture," Great-Aunt Maisie announced as she slid into the front seat of the rental car.

"Only technically," their father said.

Great-Aunt Maisie adjusted her fur coat—this one silver and even fluffier than the other one—and harrumphed.

"It was my impression you had moved to Arabia," she said.

"Qatar," their father said.

His eyes met Maisie's and Felix's in the rearview mirror, and they could see that he was amused by Great-Aunt Maisie, not offended.

The nurse was still standing uncertainly by the car with the wheelchair that had delivered Great-Aunt Maisie to them.

"What are you waiting for?" Great-Aunt Maisie said to their father.

Their father shook his head and put the car in drive. Maisie was sure that the nurse looked relieved to see them leave.

The snow fell heavier and faster as they drove down the dark Newport streets. When they turned onto Bellevue Avenue, Great-Aunt Maisie let out a little moan.

"Home," she said softly.

Her face stayed turned to look out the window.

"Penelope's house," she said, pointing to another mansion. "And Charles's." She pointed to another farther down the road.

When they headed down the long tree-lined driveway that led to the front door of Elm Medona, Great-Aunt Maisie sat up straighter.

"It always looks so beautiful in the snow," she said.

Their father let out an appreciative low whistle. "It's some house," he said.

"Well, of course it is," Great-Aunt Maisie said. "My father would only build a magnificent house. Phinneas Pickworth did nothing on a small scale."

"What does it mean?" their father said, entering the circular drive in front of the house. "Elm Medona."

Great-Aunt Maisie looked away from the window and at their father.

"Why, it's an anagram," she said. "Ask the children how much Phinneas Pickworth loved anagrams."

Felix leaned forward.

"You mean, it isn't a tree of some kind?"

Great-Aunt Maisie laughed. "You should know better than that by now," she said.

She opened the door and slowly stepped out

into the snow. Maisie and Felix watched as she raised both of her arms upward toward the sky, threw her head back, and let loose a lovely, tinkling laugh of joy.

⼟ ⼟ ⼟ ⼟ ⼟

"Five fifty-eight," their father told their mother when they entered the house.

Two maids, two butlers, and four security guards all hovered in the entrance.

"Thank you," their mother said.

She had on a long, black velvet skirt and a white, satin blouse with small, satin-covered buttons down the front. The shirt was open enough to reveal a string of pearls resting at her collar.

"You look pretty," their father said softly.

Their mother blushed and looked away from him. But Maisie and Felix sneaked smiles at each other.

One of the butlers had taken Great-Aunt Maisie's coat, and another had arrived with a silver tray with five champagne glasses.

"Three of these have the real stuff," their mother said. "And two have sparkling cider."

"Where's Great-Aunt Maisie?" Felix asked.

"Oh dear," their mother said. "She's wandered off."

They all set off in search of her, quickly locating her halfway up the Grand Staircase, staring at the picture of her younger self that hung there.

"I remember this day," she said, her gnarled finger tenderly touching the image. "It started out as such a good day. But then Thorne . . . well . . . it was the last time I spoke to my brother."

Her finger paused on Uncle Thorne's face at the edge of the picture.

"Darling," their mother said, "we have oysters and pâté and—"

Great-Aunt Maisie raised her hand and shushed her.

"Who else is here?" she asked.

Was it Maisie's imagination or did the dark sky turn even darker and the wind begin to howl?

"Just us," their mother told her. "And the staff."

Great-Aunt Maisie cocked her head to one side.

"The storm seems to be getting worse," their father said.

But Great-Aunt Maisie wasn't listening to them. Instead, she slowly began to make her way up the Grand Staircase.

Everyone rushed to follow her, their mother saying, "Darling, really, dinner is all ready."

At the top of the stairs, Great-Aunt Maisie did not even pause. She continued in her slow, regal manner down the hallway.

To Maisie's and Felix's surprise, the wall that hid the secret staircase to The Treasure Chest gaped open.

"What in the world?" their mother said.

With determination, Great-Aunt Maisie kept moving, now heading up the stairway, Maisie and Felix and their parents close behind her.

The red velvet rope that usually stretched across the door of The Treasure Chest lay unhooked and dangling.

They all stopped in the doorway.

Behind them, the wind howled still more.

Inside The Treasure Chest, a man stepped out of the shadows. He had a head full of stark-white hair, small, round wire-rimmed glasses, and the biggest, droopiest snow-white mustache that any of them had ever seen. He wore an all-white suit with a vivid red silk ascot and matching pocket square. In one hand, he held a walking stick, ebony black with a climbing snake carved into it. At the top of the stick, where his hand rested on the snake's head, two emerald eyes gleamed from it and a gold tongue protruded.

Great-Aunt Maisie gasped.

The man grinned.

"Well, well," he said.

Great-Aunt Maisie uttered just one word: "Thorne."

PEARL BUCK
June 26, 1892–March 6, 1973

Pearl Comfort Sydenstricker was born on June 26, 1892. Although she became famous for writing about rural life in China, Pearl was actually born in Hillsboro, West Virginia. Her parents, Absalom and Caroline Sydenstricker, Southern Presbyterian missionaries, were stationed in China when three of their four eldest children died in a very short span of time. Pearl's mother insisted on returning to the United States to recover from her grief. Pearl was born there, but at the age of three months, the family returned to China. She is also known by her Chinese name, Sai Zhenzhu.

The Sydenstrickers lived in Zhenjiang, a small city on the Yangtze River. Pearl's father spent most of his time away from home, trying to convert people to Christianity in the northern Chinese countryside. Pearl grew up in a household with her mother, her younger sister, Grace, and her nanny, Wang Amah. She spoke both English and Chinese fluently and was taught by a Chinese tutor, Mr. Kung. This combination of Eastern and Western beliefs and cultures influenced her for her entire life.

In 1900, during the Boxer Rebellion, Pearl, her mother, Grace, and Wang Amah fled to Shanghai. Her father stayed behind, intent on continuing his missionary work despite the danger to Westerners. However, later that year, out of fear for their safety in China, the family went back to the United States, where they lived with her mother's family in West Virginia for almost two years. They returned to China in 1902, and Pearl spent most of the next thirty years of her life there, leaving to attend Randolph-Macon Woman's College in Lynchburg, Virginia, and later to get her MA from Cornell University.

Shortly after graduation, Pearl went home to China. In 1917, she married John Lossing Buck, an agricultural economist. They moved to Nanxuzhou, a poor, rural town that inspired the stories that she would later write about life in China. A few years later, both Pearl and her husband began teaching at Nanking University in Nanking. Their first child, Carol, was born in 1921 with PKU, a genetic disorder that left her severely mentally disabled. They adopted a baby girl, Janice, four years later.

Like her mother, Pearl suffered many tragedies as an adult. She had to place her daughter Carol in an institution in New Jersey. Her mother died. And in 1927, a violent attack on Westerners known as the Nanking Incident forced the Bucks to go into hiding before they fled to Shanghai and then to Japan. This was very similar to the time when Pearl was a child and her family had to evacuate to Shanghai during the Boxer Rebellion. Shortly after the Bucks returned to China, they got divorced. But during the same time, Pearl had begun to publish stories and essays in magazines such as *The Nation*, *The Chinese Recorder*, *Asia*, and *Atlantic Monthly*. In 1930, her first novel, *East Wind, West Wind* was published.

In 1931, Pearl's second novel, *The Good Earth*, became the best-selling book of both 1931 and 1932. *The Good Earth* won the Pulitzer Prize, the William Dean Howells Medal, and was adapted into a major film. Her other books include *Sons, A House Divided, The First Wife and Other Stories, All Men are Brothers, The Mother, This Proud Heart*, and biographies of her mother and father, *The Exile* and *Fighting Angel*. In 1938, Pearl won the Nobel Prize in Literature, the first American woman to ever do so. At the time, the Nobel Committee said she won "for her rich and truly epic descriptions of peasant life in China and for her biographical masterpieces."

In 1934, conditions in China had worsened so much that Pearl decided to leave her beloved homeland and move back to the United States. To be closer to Carol, Pearl bought an old farmhouse, Green Hills Farm, in Bucks County, Pennsylvania. To her, the house's solid stone and century-old history symbolized strength and durability. She remarried and went on to adopt six more children. She and her husband founded the East and West Association, dedicated to cultural exchange and understanding between Asia and the West. During the 1930s and '40s, Asian and mixed-race children were considered unadoptable. As a response to this prejudice, Pearl established Welcome House, the first international, interracial adoption agency. Today, Welcome House has placed over five thousand children. Pearl continued her work helping with international adoptions when she founded the Pearl S. Buck Foundation in 1964. It provides sponsorship funding for thousands of Amerasian children in Asia.

Pearl Buck died in March 1973. She is buried at Green Hills Farm, which is used as the center for the Pearl S. Buck Foundation.

The adventure continues in

THE
TREASURE
·CHEST·

No. 4
Prince of Air

Even though Felix landed hard, his back crashing onto a wooden floor, he oddly still had the sensation of moving. Moving slowly. Upward.

He opened his eyes and saw a sea of high-button boots, long skirts, and stiff trousers.

"Little boy," a woman with a feathered hat scolded. "Get back up here or you'll fly off."

Felix pulled his aching self up to a sitting position. He was facing about a dozen people sitting on a wooden bench, staring down at him.

He grinned up at them and took the hand of a man with a mustache even bigger than Great-Uncle Thorne's, letting the man help him to his feet. Everyone scrunched over so that he could squeeze in.

In the distance, Felix saw the ocean glittering bright blue. That combined with the sky, equally as blue and sprinkled with perfect white, fluffy clouds, made him feel as if he had landed smack into the middle of a postcard. A postcard that was definitely going up a hill along a creaky track. The people around him looked like they had stepped out of a postcard, too, with their big hats and suits and funny shoes.

A few of the women were holding hands tight and staring all wide-eyed and scared.

"It's my first time," one of them said. She had hair in big, bouncy banana curls, and the tip of her nose was sunburned.

"Mine too," the dark-haired one beside her said in a quivering voice.

Felix nodded at them as if he understood. Shifting his gaze in the other direction, away from the ocean, he saw a giant, fake elephant. There appeared to be people standing on top of it.

The car reached the top, paused, then coasted down the track.

Everyone, except Felix, screamed or gasped or laughed nervously.

Felix smiled. Wherever he had landed, this was a roller coaster. The slowest roller coaster he'd ever been on.

Maisie's head popped out from between the legs of the banana-curled girl and the dark-haired girl.

"What was that?" she said, laughing.

The man with the giant mustache glared at her.

"Young lady," he said. "You have just taken a ride on the Gravity Pleasure Switchback Railroad."

"I have?" she said, scrambling to her feet.

The roller coaster had come to a stop, and

everyone was getting out. But instead of leaving the ride, they were getting into another car.

The girl with the banana curls fanned herself wildly. "I thought I was going to faint," she said. "Didn't you?"

Her dark-haired friend nodded and wiped her forehead with a small, white handkerchief.

Maisie and Felix tried not to laugh as they followed them out of the car and onto another one.

"Now what?" Maisie asked.

"We're switching tracks," a woman explained. "So that we can go up that hill."

Once again, the car crept up a hill along a wooden track, going slower than the speed limit on Thames Street back in Newport. Once again, it paused at the top and then made its rickety way down. As the people around them screamed and closed their eyes, Maisie and Felix laughed.

A few summers ago, their father had taken them to Coney Island, where they'd ridden an old wooden roller coaster called The Cyclone. Felix, terrified, could only do it once. But Maisie and their father rode it over and over again, her squeals filling the salty amusement park air. Their father had told them that at the turn of the twentieth century, amusement parks were built at seaside resorts, like Coney Island and Atlantic

City and all along the coast of New England. Most of those parks were long gone now, he'd said. A lot of them were destroyed by fires because everything in them was made of wood. Others had closed due to neglect. Surely they were in one of them right now.

Felix studied the clothes of the people sitting on the bench with them. Yes, they looked like people from the turn of the century. And there was the ocean in the distance. He even heard the sound of music that played on merry-go-rounds.

The car came to a halt, and everyone stood to disembark.

Maisie grabbed Felix's arm and pointed to the words written in lights across an arch.

"How did we get so lucky?" she said.

Felix read the words out loud.

"Coney Island," he said.

To time travel and land in an amusement park—and not just any amusement park but an amusement park in New York—made Maisie about as happy as she could be. Not only could they ride rides all day (although she hoped the other rides were better than that lame roller coaster), eat hot dogs, and walk on the beach, but she could pretend she lived back here and at the end of the day get on the J train and head home.

Almost a perfect day. Except for one thing: Where were Great-Aunt Maisie and Great-Uncle Thorne?

If she asked Felix, he would get all worried, and there would go their day of fun. He would want to find them, and instead of getting on— Maisie tried to take in everything she was seeing and decide what to do next—there! That Ferris wheel over there. Instead of riding that, they would have to walk up and down looking for two cranky, old people.

"Look!" she said to her brother. "Let's go on the Ferris wheel."

The sign in front of it said: WORLD'S LARGEST FERRIS WHEEL. Which it wasn't. The thing had only twelve cars and moved excruciatingly slow.

Still, she grabbed Felix's arm and pulled him toward it. Her plan, she decided, was to keep him too busy to wonder about Great-Aunt Maisie and Great-Uncle Thorne. Eventually, they would find whomever they needed to find, give him or her the handcuffs, then go back home. For all they knew, Great-Aunt Maisie and Great-Uncle Thorne were still standing in the auditorium at Anne Hutchinson Middle School fighting over the handcuffs.

Maisie stopped suddenly.

The handcuffs. Who had the handcuffs? She didn't. She lifted her hands in front of her face just to be sure. Her black, tulle, magician's assistant skirt didn't have any pockets, and neither did the old leotard she had on from her misguided efforts at a ballet class last year. The thing had small pills all over it and was just tight enough to be uncomfortable and ride up her butt. No pockets there.

She glanced at Felix who was staring at The Roundabout with a worried expression. Maybe he had the handcuffs in his pocket. But if she asked him that, and he didn't have them, then he would get worried about how they were ever going to get home and their day would be ruined. Maisie sighed over all the things she had to keep quiet about so that Felix would stay calm.

"World's largest Ferris wheel!" she said, continuing toward it.

This time, Felix took her arm and stopped her.

"Wait a minute," he said. "We have to pay for a ride."

He pointed to a sign.

"Five cents, to be exact," he said.

Of course they had to pay, Maisie scolded herself. How could she be so dumb? Somehow they had to find some money. She wasn't going to be at Coney Island on a beautiful day and not ride the rides.

Maisie's face brightened.

"Uh-oh," Felix said. Clearly she'd come up with a scheme that he would no doubt not want to be part of.

"Do you have your cards with you?" she asked.

"Yes," he said carefully.

"Well then, we'll have to get to work, won't we?" Maisie told him.

Performing card tricks on the runway of Coney Island was one of the last things Felix wanted to do. But he recognized that determination in his sister's eyes. No matter what he said, he would never be able to convince her that this was a bad idea.

He took the deck of cards from his jacket pocket, shuffled them, and said, "Ladies and gentlemen, what I have here is an ordinary deck of cards . . ."

An hour later, Maisie and Felix had two dollars and twenty-five cents, and they were sitting in one of the wooden cars on the Ferris wheel, slowly rotating upward.

"You promised we could go on The Roundabout," Felix reminded Maisie.

They were standing on top of a giant, wooden

elephant called The Elephant Colossus. They'd
already gone inside its legs. One had a cigar
store and the other sold postcards. The body of
the elephant was a hotel, and here, twelve stories
up, was an observation deck where they could
look down on the runway, which throbbed with
people.

Dusk had settled over Coney Island. The
beach beyond the amusement park was still
crowded. People splashed in the ocean beneath a
reddish-orange sky.

"I know," Maisie said. "It's just hard to get
enthusiastic about a merry-go-round."

"I went on The Serpentine Railroad with
you," he said. "Three times."

The Serpentine Railroad was the other roller
coaster. It went all of twelve miles an hour, twice
as fast as The Switchback but still eternally slow.
Felix had started to enjoy the slower pace of the
rides, how the Ferris wheel took almost twenty
minutes to go around, and how the roller coasters
felt like rides in a convertible, the wind blowing
on his face and the salty ocean air mixed with the
smell of hot dogs roasting and the pungent oil
they used to grease the tracks.

Those hot dogs. Felix had eaten three. And
two Italian ices sold by a man in a straw hat and

red-and-white-striped jacket. He played a strange instrument that he told them was called a hurdy-gurdy. It had strings and a keyboard, and the man cranked it to make music that sounded almost like bagpipes. As he played it, a skinny, little monkey with big eyes danced in front of him.

Thinking about it made Felix hungry again. He smiled to himself. What a perfect day this had been. He had been careful not to mention the fact that they had no idea where Great-Aunt Maisie or Great-Uncle Thorne might be. Maybe they were out there somewhere in that crowd waiting in line to ride the Ferris wheel or enter one of the sideshows. Maybe they were back in Newport at Anne Hutchinson Middle School. Felix knew that if he speculated as to their whereabouts with Maisie, she would get mad at him for ruining the day. He could almost hear her grumbling about those old people getting in the way of a perfect summer day at Coney Island.

Wait a minute, Felix thought. *A perfect summer day?*

"Maisie?" he said.

"Okay, okay, we'll go on the merry-go-round."

"Wasn't the Talent Show in March?" he asked.

She narrowed her eyes at him. "That rhetorical question is supposed to make me realize something, right?"

Felix opened his arms wide. "It's definitely summer here."

"So?" she said.

She hated when he figured something out before she did. What did it matter that the Talent Show was in March, and it was summer here at Coney Island in 18 . . . 18-whatever?

"Sir?" Felix said, turning to the man beside him. "What's today's date?"

The man laughed. "Why? Do you have an important engagement?"

"As a matter-of-fact," Felix said. "I kind of do."

The man furrowed his dark eyebrows. "It is June 18, 1894."

With slow, deliberate motions, the man pulled a very large pocket watch from his vest pocket.

"And," he added, "it is seven seventeen in the evening."

He wiggled his eyebrows and turned back to his conversation.

"How could we have traveled to a different day?" Felix blurted.